Praise for 1

Michael Loyd Gray's prose un.
cadence of a

~Stuart Dybek, author of I Sailed with Magellan
and Coast of Chicago

*A gritty take on Americana weaved together by
a master storyteller. Busted Flat is a harsh exploration
of falling through society's cracks. On the Road
meets Last Exit to Brooklyn.*

~Anthony Squiers, author of An Introduction to the Social
and Political Philosophy of Bertolt Brecht

*Busted Flat is a witty, gritty coming of age story, tracking a
young runaway's choices when he realizes that his mentor-
in-crime is a ticking time bomb. Between his PTSD and
escalating violence, Shiner's unraveling and Hap's hesitation
to set off on his own create a suspenseful portrait of the
fringes where family takes many forms. Told in fast-paced
flash-fiction chapters, this is an exciting novel that shows
us moments in time from a compelling and
complex underworld of American society.*

~Carol Burbank, Storyweaving

*Busted Flat is a gripping tale of the adventurous survival of
non-prominence reminiscent of Huckleberry Finn.
Mister Clemens would approve.*

~W. G. Griffiths, author of Malchus

Busted Flat

A Flash Novella

By Michael Loyd Gray

BLUE
CEDAR
PRESS

Blue Cedar Press
Wichita, Kansas

Busted Flat: a flash novella
Copyright © 2024 by Michael Loyd Gray

Blue Cedar Press PO Box 48715
Wichita, KS 67201
Visit the Blue Cedar Press website: www.bluecedarpress.com
10 9 8 7 6 5 4 3 2 1

First edition October 2024
ISBN: 978-1-958728-29-1 (paper)
ISBN: 978-1-958728-30-7 (ebook)

Cover art by Katie Gantt
Cover and interior design by Gina Laiso, Integrita Productions
Editor Laura Tillem and Gretchen Eick

"Air Boy," appeared in Ginosko Review.

"The Hard Winter" appeared in OpenDoor Magazine.

The chapter titled "Finders, Keepers," appeared in The Mantelpiece, in Iceland.

"Tumbleweeds" appeared in The Exacting Clam.

"Expendable" appeared in WINK.

"Graceland" appeared in Timada's Diary, a journal in Khazakstan.

The concluding chapter of the novella, "Busted Flat in Baton Rouge," appeared in Burningword Literary Journal.

"Birthday" appeared in SamFiftyFour.

Library of Congress Control Number: 2024942126
Printed in the United States of America at IngramSpark.

"If you don't know where you're going,
any road will take you there."

~George Harrison

AIR BOY

I was born in the air. Literally. Somewhere over Ohio, so I was told. A few miles straight up. Among the clouds. Literally. An air boy. If I had a memory of it, which I don't, maybe I'd remember white, puffy clouds lingering outside the plane's windows. Or the faces of passengers sneaking looks at the fuss I created with my dramatic entrance.

But my first memories began much later. I certainly don't remember the hospital in Kalamazoo, Michigan, where I was taken when the plane landed, and where I was declared a Michigan resident. But now, when I look at the sky, I think all of it stretching everywhere as far as can be seen is where I'm from.

I'm not bound by soil at all.

My folks – well, that's another matter. They weren't air people at all. They were consumed by fire. Roasted alive when my father tried to beat a train to a crossing and lost the bet. They had been drunk, of course, and so they were alcohol people as well as fire people. One fueled the other.

Then they became ash people.

I heard a song on a radio say fire is the devil's only friend.

I was cycled through various foster homes but never could find a good fit and so I always escaped. On the lam seemed to be my natural state. That cycle went on until grandparents stepped up and said they'd take a crack at it. But they were ancient and nearly broke except for Social Security. I got tired of pork and beans and hamburger helper in a double-wide trailer surrounded by other old folks waiting for death.

How I got my name – Hap – is a good story, I suppose. Everybody on the plane that day said I just sort of "happened." The boy who just happened on the back seat of a plane over Youngstown, Ohio. For a few days, my mom called me the boy who happened and then she shortened it to Hap because she liked how abrupt it sounds. But I don't think about it as a name. That's just what I know, who I am – Hap.

Hap who happened.

When I met Shiner, while I panhandled on the streets, he said Hap was a dipshit name for a kid, but he took me in anyway. He was a hard man, a veteran of Afghanistan, his only soft spot apparently for kids like me who struggled to live off what the streets provided. That had happened to him, too, he said. He knew what it was like to go hungry and sleep without a bed in some alley under a leaky awning. He was a man, like me, who just happened, I reckon.

So, I was along for the ride. No jumping off. It was too late for that.

"You ride with Jesse James," Shiner says, "and you are Jesse James."

It all just happened, like that day in the air over Ohio.

THE HARD WINTER

Just past Kalamazoo, we saw a small town and Shiner eyeballed glowing houses roosting alongside the dark highway. Whenever he got focused like that, and graveyard quiet, I knew trouble was brewing, like when we abruptly stole the truck the day before in Detroit.

He pulled onto the shoulder for a better look at a house up a rise. It was set back among trees. We saw lights from other houses, but they were a good half mile down the road.

"I reckon that's the one," Shiner said, excitement in his voice.

"The one for what?"

"For dinner and gas money, stupid."

I looked at the house, light pouring from its large front window, the drapes open, but I didn't see anybody. Shiner got out and I thought of just staying in the truck, but he stopped and stared at me, waiting until I got out and fell into line like a good little soldier.

It was so Shiner to just knock on the damn door, shove a gun in the face of the old man who answered, and barge right past him. Shiner made the old man's wife, a tiny, gray-haired gal, make us cheeseburgers and fries drowning in ketchup. We ate quickly, the old folks cowering in a corner of the kitchen. When he was done, Shiner robbed them, but it wasn't much of a take.

Shiner leaned in and whispered in my ear. I can't say I was surprised by it.

"But they're just old folks, man," I said, glancing at them. "Senior citizens, for fuck's sake."

"They've got eyes and mouths, don't they?"

Shiner shot that look like a drill boring into me and then disappeared out the back door. It shut loudly, like the bang of a gun. I looked back at these two old people huddled together, clutching each other on their knees, shaking and tears running down their gray faces.

They reminded me of my own grandparents, and I pulled my gun and fired two shots through their front window. They automatically keeled over, flopping like fish on a dock.

Their old eyes pleaded for mercy, and I fired a third shot at the window, for Shiner's benefit. One – or both -- of the old folks had shit their britches and the smell was awful. It filled the room, and I nearly threw up. When I caught up to Shiner, he smoked a cigarette real casual-like.

"Well, numbnuts?" he said.

"Well, what?"

I looked at the ground a moment and I think he took that as guilt, confirmation.

"Okay, then," he said, nodding.

The wind came up. It was strong. A chill was in the air and it felt like it could snow. Shiner walked ahead of me in the tall grass, like nothing happened at all, and I thought briefly of just ending it there, maybe see if I could find the exit to this waking nightmare. I even put my hand on the butt of my gun. But I hadn't worked up enough nerve yet. I suppose I still believed in salvation.

As we merged with the stream of traffic, I glanced once over my shoulder at the house, light pouring out the shattered front window. I could see someone looking out. I couldn't tell which of the old folks it was. It didn't matter. Their faces were already fading.

But I thought, they really need to fix that window before the hard winter sets in.

JUDGMENT DAY

I thought some more about shooting Shiner. But not so much as a plan. It was more like – could I even do it? Why should I? Is there a point to that? He'd glance at me with those cold eyes while he drove us across the tip of Indiana toward Chicago, and I wondered if he had any idea at all what I was thinking.

I wondered what the fuck he was thinking.

By the time the Chicago skyline came into sight on the horizon, I'd replayed in my head dozens of times what happened back at that Michigan house with those old folks. How scared they were while Shiner robbed them and pushed them around. How faded they looked, like ancient ghosts. How ordinary their run-down little house was.

Grubby, really.

The old lady whimpered like a beat dog when Shiner took her wedding ring. He wasn't kind about it and hurt her finger. Then he ripped a necklace off her neck. She bawled like a hungry baby. The husband just stared at the floor and shook.

Shiner got us to downtown Chicago, to the Gold Coast, he called it, and we went for deep dish at a place called Lou Malnati's. I'd never been to Chi-Town. That's what Shiner called it. I'd never had any deep dish, either. It was awfully thick. But damn good. Just one slice of it was like a whole meal. I felt like I could live on it for a while. Deep dish was better than the greasy cheeseburgers Shiner had made that old couple fix for us.

I drank a second beer, and then a third, something tasty called Goose Island, and I thought for a moment about those old people. They were paying for our deep dish, our Goose Island, and for whatever room Shiner would find us for the night. I struggled with the morality of it. Like with them street boys back in Detroit, I guess those old folks were competition for food, too. Survival.

But it's not like they didn't survive, too, the old folks. I let them off the hook. That was down to me. But I don't know why it should be that way, in my hands. Maybe that was the price of my ride with Shiner. Did he want me along to do dirty work? That thing back with the old folks was some kind of fucked up test, I reckon. Did I pass? How did morality figure into it? I was thinking that morality might be simpler than what people think. That it's knowing what you feel good about and what you don't. A feeling. That's morality.

Someone like Shiner might not know the difference, might not feel good and bad and just always felt neutral, I suppose. He might not know how he really felt. That would mess with his ability to know morality. Maybe block it altogether.

Anyway, that's what went through my head as I dug into another slice of deep dish. I vaguely hoped that when it came time for judgment day, that those poor old people would remember what I'd done for them.

A MAN HUNGRY FOR SOIL

I think Shiner was once a man of soil, with solid roots dug down deep – before the Army and the lack of morality of Afghanistan, where he was uprooted and re-assembled, parts jammed back together like splintered bricks making a sagging ragged wall.

Once back home from war, the wall must have tumbled and now he's a sort of withering, flighty vine twisting in the wind, time running out, desperate to take hold somewhere that might make sense. A man hungry for the stability of deep rich soil again. Maybe his roots are dead from lack of soil. A rootless tumbleweed of a man with a temper that can go off sudden-like, like a whistling teapot.

I saw that for myself the day we met, as I rummaged dumpsters behind a McDonald's in Detroit. I hadn't eaten well in a while and not at all for nearly two days and so I jumped right into the dumpster with two other street boys. I figured they'd understand. Brothers in arms and all that streetwise bullshit. But when we climbed out with some rancid fries and a few stale pieces of burger buns, they beat me up and took my food.

Shiner was getting into his truck, which was stolen, and saw our commotion and ran over and beat one of the boys so bad the kid lay still on the pavement with blood pouring off his head and out of his mouth. I figured he was dead. I'll never know because we peeled out of McDonald's and I didn't look back. We left Detroit behind and wound up at a diner outside Ypsilanti. There was a men's room on the side of the diner and Shiner tossed me a towel, bar of soap, and a shirt from his bag.

"Go clean up. That's a rule before you can sit down to eat with me."

I smelled the bar of soap. I hadn't smelled soap in a while. It had a clean, lime aroma. I held it to my nose.

"Go wash with it, boy – don't eat it."

"Why are you doing this," I said, wondering if he was queer. "Why are you helping me?"

He looked off, at the setting sun, meaty hands on his hips.

"I don't know. But I am. Okay? Don't look a gift horse, numbnuts.

"I don't know what that means, gift horse. Or numbnuts, either."

"Never mind that. It don't mean much."

"Then why say it?"

He frowned.

"Just finish up and come inside. Or run off, like you're used to. Your choice, boy."

In the men's room, I washed my face, hair, and armpits with soap and slipped on the shirt, a thick flannel one that would finally give me some winter layering under my thin jacket and t-shirt. When I went inside the diner, he looked surprised to see me.

"Figured you for a runner, boy."

I shrugged and looked around, smelling warm food. A variety of pleasant odors.

"I'm hungry."

"Hunger makes us all practical," Shiner said.

I wondered what he might want but forced myself not to think about it while I ate roast beef and mashed potatoes still simmering in brown gravy, steam rising off them. The meal and the price for it, I knew, were two separate issues. One damn thing at a time.

"Did you kill that boy?" I said after we ate.

He looked out the window. It was already dark. There was nothing to see except lights from a semi-trailer truck. He was a large man. Not tall but muscular—husky, I guess is the word for it.

"Does it matter?" he finally said, still staring into darkness.

I wasn't sure how to answer the question myself. But that boy he beat down was competition for food. Band of brothers be damned. There aren't no brothers when you're hungry. That's what it came down to – survival.

I thought about going to the men's room and then skipping out, maybe try and hitch a ride back to Detroit. But the roast beef and potatoes were speaking to me. My belly was full and warm. I'd gotten a taste and wanted more. Craved it.

The decision to ride with Shiner a while and see where that went was no more complicated than that.

RUNNER

I reckon I've always been a runner. I ran off into snowy woods squealing like a beat dog when I was just a little kid and they told me my folks were gone. All burned up. Not coming back ever. Just ashes and charred bone to be scooped together into a pot.

I vaguely recall the funeral. The closed casket. The silence. The musty smell of the church. I remember well the gray-faced man of God preaching words that didn't mean anything to me, that sounded like he was talking about people and places and ideas that didn't exist. Fantasies about the meaning of life – and death – was all I took from that deal.

I clearly remember the pissy pained looks from other kids when I arrived at a state center, which is a polite way of saying jail for kids waiting for foster homes. The other kids were a pack of hungry wolves eyeing new meat. Licking their chops as they looked me over up and down and stood apart in their pack, baring teeth like a wolf would. I was competition for food, for attention – for a home.

A threat.

The first foster home was at least decent, the house clean and warm during a cold winter. The food was okay, I suppose – potatoes and mystery meat were often the special. Runny chili with too many beans and not enough meat. At least the potatoes were done a variety of ways, and I liked mashed best with thick brown gravy.

But the middle-aged couple who took me in were settled into their routines. I figured they thought helping me was a "Christian" thing to do, but they probably hadn't bargained for apathy – for resistance. I think they supposed they'd put the Bible in front of me and Jesus would magically take over and I'd fall into line. They weren't abusive people, but they weren't warm, either. Neutral. Resigned to an obligation they'd taken on but with no idea how to do it.

So, I ran as soon as winter let up a little. I had no plan, no destination. My jacket was too light when a late snow came, and I begged at a house. That lady fed me peanut butter sandwiches on stale bread while she called the law. I was taken back to the state center. When you run like that, because you have no idea where or what your true home is, you don't consider the consequences. They pop into the picture later.

The kids at the center laughed at me when I was brought back in. The wolf pack gave me the finger and called me names – called me a loser. When the social workers weren't around, one of the wolves called me "asswipe" and shoved me and I beat him to the ground, drawing on repressed anger, I suppose, and they had to put a few stiches in his forehead. They locked me in a room with just a cot and toilet for a week. All it did was sharpen my desire to run. It built up more anger.

It took some time for the social workers to find me another home, folks willing to take a chance on a runner who'd already used his fists. That couple was younger, in their thirties, and the lady couldn't have kids. So, I became their fantasy project, I guess. They were right and proper Christians, too.

But that lady couldn't cook worth a lick. I'd say her best dish was boiling spaghetti and drowning it with Ragu sauce. It was spaghetti night too often, and I even got the shits once from it. The spaghetti lady didn't really know how to talk to me, and her husband, a construction worker who clammed up and hid in his beer bottle once he got home off the job, had only gone along with the project because it was what she wanted. To him, I was just competition for food, I suppose. For attention.

A threat.

So, I ran again.

That time, I managed to stay on the lam a couple days, just wandering neighborhoods and sleeping in weeds or under a tree. I felt sort of free, but it was the freedom of being cast adrift. I ate green apples and got rained on, too. The apples gave me the shits. Hunger got me caught again.

Back at the state center, that boy I beat teamed up with the rest of the wolf pack and they gave me a beating to remember. I got a cracked rib and broken nose and spent a few days in a hospital and when I went back to the center, it was back to the locked room with a cot and toilet to separate me from the others. Solitary confinement, like in a prison.

I reckon the center was desperate when they reached out to my grandparents, who'd at first declined to take me on. I wasn't eager for it, either. I barely knew them. But like the all the other foster couples, they deemed themselves good Christians who had to finally respond to the call, no matter how lousy they'd be at it.

I guess because my old folks were kin, I compromised and stuck it out. I was a runner, but it hadn't gotten me anywhere yet. Food was always the problem. My grandma could cook okay, and her spaghetti didn't give me the shits. That was enough to slow me down for a while.

Decent food and few rules kept me there. There was no Bible and no lectures on morality. They glued themselves to their TV most nights and I lived in my room, reading comics. They were relieved I could fend for myself. Soon I made my own meals and then theirs, too. Control shifted ever so slightly. That was new to me—control.

I made it to high school, but I was a poor student. My teachers said I was surprisingly bright and even perceptive but distracted. I guess I was still expecting my parents to magically re-assemble from dead ashes to flesh and appear around the next corner.

By my junior year, I fell into a gang of boys who had taken to the streets because their lives were full of distraction and disappointment, too, and they couldn't get along with parents. So, they became runners, like me. By then, I knew it was pathetic bullshit to think you'd ever see your dead parents again. Not on this Earth, not in any heaven.

One of those boys I ran with died from drugs. Another died because he was too slow jumping across tracks in front of a train. It reminded me too much of what happened to my parents and after that I set off on my own on the streets, a solitary runner, staying dirty, maybe sleeping huddled together with somebody on cold nights in alleys or abandoned houses.

Then Shiner came along and when I hopped in the truck with him, I reckon I was running yet again.

But with someone more like me than anybody else because he doesn't know where he's running to, or why. He just knows running is not standing still, where maybe something catches up to you.

I'm a runner.

TUMBLEWEEDS

I don't know that Shiner can stop killing. Not for good, anyway. It seems like he can put it on pause a while, maybe even for long spells of time, but then eventually something overcomes him. Just washes over him like an ocean wave. I reckon it's a curse he picked up in Afghanistan, the killing. A demon inside him.

I don't know why he couldn't just leave his demon in Afghanistan. But there might not even be a why. Probably not. It just is. A lot of the world just is. No rhyme or reason, especially the reason part. I came into this world to dirt poor parents roasted in a fiery car crash. I know a little bit about hard luck.

I've asked Shiner about Afghanistan, about what happened to him there, but he gives me the cold blue eyes glare. It speaks louder than words.

"Mind your own damn business, Hap," he hisses. "You hear me?"

I know to clam up because one day he might kill me, too. That's just a notion on my part. But I think I'm not immune to his dark side. Nobody is. I'm expendable, at some point. Maybe to just eventually be cast aside. No longer of use. Dropped off by the side of a road in the middle of nowhere – or worse. These are things I know and still I stick with Shiner. I don't know why. I think in America there's a whole bunch of folks who can't afford to ask a lot of whys. I reckon that's my tribe.

Shiner took me in when no one else would. I reckon he saw a little of himself, before Afghanistan, in me. I don't know that for a fact. He'd never say it was so, of course. He doesn't say much at all.

His eyes do a lot of the talking, those steel blue eyes that can flash hot or cold. I kind of fell into line behind him because it got me out of sleeping in alleys and away from perverts. But I don't think Shiner's that way – a pervert. He don't come across like that. He keeps his hands – and words – to himself.

Now we're just rambling men, I guess. Tumbleweeds. Drifters in a stolen pickup and living off burgers and pizza when Shiner scores money, mostly from stealing or robbing a gas station, but at least I'm out of the rain and so I ain't complaining. Maybe I'm a voice when he wants to hear one, which ain't often.

I said tumbleweeds again, more to just myself, and Shiner says, "What about them?"

"I've never seen any."

"They just a weed, boy."

A few miles go by. I say, "But they don't have roots."

He looked at me.

"Because they dead, boy. They don't have no damn use for roots."

I look away and dropped the subject. That was the longest conversation we'd had in days. Shiner suddenly turns onto a highway, and I see we're headed west.

"Where to now, Shiner?"

"I reckon Arizona," he says after a moment.

"How come?"

"Well, you want to see some damn tumbleweeds, don't you, boy?"

I nod, thinking it was the nicest thing Shiner had said to me in a long time.

CRATER

We're looking at a humongous meteor crater outside Winslow, Arizona. Tourists with cameras and kids swirling around us, like me and Shiner are islands in a human river. People from all over the world by the sound and look of it. Funny sounding languages. Lots of little smiling Japanese people. I'd never seen Japanese before. They seemed awfully polite.

Shiner abruptly sings lyrics from some song under his breath, almost a whisper, like he didn't want anybody to realize he knew the song. He says it's a famous song. By some band I never even heard of. From back in his day. Something about standing on a corner in Winslow, and a flat-bed truck and some girl. Beats hell out of me. I saw the town, Winslow, and it wasn't nothing to write home about.

But the meteor crater's the biggest damn hole I ever saw or could imagine.

"Well, you ain't seen the Grand Canyon yet, boy," Shiner says quietly as he stares into the crater.

"We headed that way?" I was curious to see an even bigger hole in the ground. I never know where we're going until Shiner decides. He's the captain and I'm crew. We're a ship, sometimes, without a rudder.

"Maybe," Shiner says. "We'll see, boy. But first, we need more money."

He looks around to see if anyone is listening in.

There's this tour guide guy talking to a small crowd of tourists about the crater. I think, yeah, we're tourists, too, me and Shiner. I'd never been a tourist before, not anywhere for anything at all. I learned that the meteor crashed during an ice age and the crater is three-quarters of a mile wide and 750 feet deep. It's a hell of a hole. I couldn't stop looking at it. Neither could Shiner. Neither could all the little Japanese people crowding the railing alongside us.

After a while, Shiner watches this Japanese family, like he's tracking them. That's how it starts when Shiner is zeroing in on a score. He has some kind of internal radar for finding scores. These Japanese folks have a couple cameras that look expensive. They took a bunch of pictures and then sat the cameras on a table. Mistake. When they go to the railing for a better look at the crater, Shiner doesn't hesitate. He swoops in like a hawk and sweeps up the cameras and we jump in the truck and barrel down the dusty road back to the highway.

"I know a place in Phoenix where we'll get good money for them," Shiner says.

I lift one and look through the lens. I think maybe it's the first camera I've ever held, and this one is a doozy.

"But can we develop the pictures first?"

Shiner glances at me, that standard cold blue glare of his, like he's trying to solve some kind of math problem and having no luck. Then his face softens ever so slightly. He's just a thief today and not a killer.

"Okay, boy. I reckon we can do that."

After we turn onto the highway, Shiner says, "What do you want them pictures for?"

"I don't know," I say, shrugging and then looking through the camera lens again, at the desert. "I never had none of my own."

Wind comes up. I look through the lens, at tumbleweeds rolling along, and push the button.

I hope the pictures don't come out blurry.

CELL PHONE

Shiner says we must see a guy in Phoenix. A fence. I didn't know what that was. The guy was old and gray and ran a pawn shop in a sleazy part of town where there were lots of rundown buildings and some of those droopy saguaros. I coaxed Shiner into snapping a photo of me under one of the big cactuses, its giant arms looking like they were waving at somebody.

The cameras we stole from that Japanese family back in Winslow fetched money for a few days. Grub and gas. That was how it was: Shiner scores and we keep going. Where? He figured that out. I was the just the co-pilot, not allowed to touch the wheel. Or, navigator, when he had a rare moment of wanting conversation.

We developed the camera's film at one of those while you wait places and then went to the food court at a mall. Shiner liked food courts. He liked Asian food. And he liked how it was always big and open and crowded – easier to blend in.

"What do you want with those damn photos, Hap?" he said, looking around. He always watched his six, as he called it.

I shrugged and looked at the first one. The Japanese family, mama and papa and two kids, smiled at the camera from the railing of that meteor crater in Winslow. They looked happy.

"I never had any photos, Shiner."

"Yeah? Well, what freaking good are those doing you, boy?"

"I just wanted to see them."

"It ain't your family."

"I know that."

"And you sure as hell ain't Japanese."

"I know I ain't Japanese. Duh? Look at my eyes. Look at my blond hair."

"I've seen blond Japanese," he says.

"No way. Really?"

"They dye it, numbnuts."

I thumbed through the photos. I never had a happy family. None of my foster homes were like that. That's why I escaped.

"They look happy, Shiner."

"Well, good for them."

I held the photo up for him.

"But they weren't too damn pleased when they saw their cameras were gone, numbnuts."

I put the photos in the envelope and slipped them into a pocket. After we ate, I glanced around at people on cell phones. Some of them ate while talking on their phones. Everybody seemed to have one.

"I've never had a cell phone, Shiner."

He wiped his mouth with a napkin.

"Who the fuck would you call?"

I shrugged.

"I reckon I don't know."

"Who the fuck could you call?" he says. "Who would call you?"

"Do you have one?"

"They could track us that way."

I saw a kid at another table, a guy maybe eighteen or less, about my age, talking on his phone. He smiled while he talked. Maybe it was his girlfriend, telling him she loved him. I never really had a girlfriend.

"But it would be nice to have a cell phone," I said.

"For fuck's sake," Shiner says. He looks around, his thief radar kicking in. "Go over to the doors and wait for me, boy."

From the doors I watched him browse the crowd, cruising the tables. Then he came over to me and handed me a cell phone after he took the battery out.

"There you go, numbnuts – now you got a freaking cell phone."

I smiled every time I felt it in my jacket pocket.

I'M TURNING JAPANESE I REALLY THINK SO

I wake up from a fitful nap and don't know where we are. Shiner says it don't much matter where, making sure to call me "numbnuts" for the millionth time, but finally he tells me it's somewhere in west Texas. Not far from Lubbock. He says that's where Buddy Holly's from.

"Who?"

"A rock and roller. Well before your time, numbnuts."

"Everything's before my time."

"Most of it, for sure, boy."

After a couple minutes of looking at dry and endless brown west Texas, I say, "How come I never heard of this Buddy Holly?"

"Because he's dead. Has been a million years. And because I reckon your generation don't know shit about history and listens to that rap horseshit."

"Just how did this Holly boy die?"

"Plane crash."

I thought about how I was born in a plane, over Youngstown, Ohio. If it had crashed, I reckon I'd never even known I'd been alive. I tell Shiner that and he laughs. I can't remember him ever laughing. His laugh is high-pitched, sort of like a girl. His laugh doesn't seem to fit a killer. I suppose killers sound like anybody else.

"Boy, when you die, it no longer matters you lived."

"Is that what you learned in Afghanistan?"

He gives me the side glance, the cold blue steel eyes.

"Don't you never mind about that, Hap. Ain't your business."

I turn on the radio and he flashes the side glance but I can tell he's okay with it.

"Maybe this Holly dude is on the radio," I say.

"Probably not. And you'd need a classic rock station."

We can't find Buddy Holly anywhere on the dial but after a while I hear a song that is one of the weirdest I've heard. It's called "Turning Japanese."

"Damn," Shiner says. "I remember this one."

The song reminds me of the photos we developed, from those cameras we stole back in Winslow, Arizona, at the famous meteor crater. The money we got from fencing them in Phoenix has us back on the road, headed nowhere but making good progress toward it.

I pull the packet of photos from a pocket and thumb through all the shots of the smiling, happy Japanese family.

Shiner shakes his head.

"I don't know what you get from them fucking photos, boy. They ain't your goddamn family."

But I think it's possible to find family almost anywhere, even in photos. You just have to wish it and it can come true. I put the photos back in the packet and keep it in my jacket pocket, close to my beating heart.

"Numbnuts," Shiner says, shaking his head.

I smile and sing, "I'm turning Japanese, I'm turning Japanese I really think so."

A TINY SEED

There's a huge thingamajig outside the Buddy Holly Center in Lubbock. I reckon you'd call it a sculpture. It's a big old pair of glasses nearly as tall as me. You could fit your body behind just one lens. I do that and Shiner looks around to see if anyone's paying attention. Checking his six, which he learned in Afghanistan. That and how to kill.

Shiner likes crowds of people so that we blend in. I don't know if anybody's looking for us yet, but Shiner says that's a given. Never assume your six is clear. But today we're just having us some fun. Spending our take from the stolen cameras before it's time to score again and hit the road. The road to nowhere, I've been calling it. Up ahead, I see a statue of Mr. Holly himself. He's wearing dorky black frame glasses just like the sculpture.

"What's with them geeky glasses?" I tell Shiner.

"That was his look. The Buddy look."

"He's kind of a funny looking dude," I say, eyeing the statue.

"Yeah, Hap? You ever look in a mirror, numbnuts?"

We go inside and listen to Mr. Holly's music. He does something with his voice. Mr. Holly sort of stutters when he sings. But it grabs you. I don't know why but it just does. In one song, he's got this girlfriend Peggy Sue and she's causing him heartache. He wants her, but I reckon she's far away or something like that. I've never heard of anyone named Peggy Sue in my whole life.

On the way out, we peek in the gift shop. I buy glasses just like Mr. Holly's. Heavy black frames. I think I look okay in them. Older.

"Just like Buddy," the smiling young and blond salesclerk says.

"Megadork," Shiner says, but softly, and I think he's just kidding me.

I call the salesclerk Peggy Sue, even though her nametag says Sylvia.

"I reckon we're all Peggy Sue here," she says. "Have a blessed day – Buddy."

We go out into the bright sunshine. I feel somehow different in my Buddy glasses, like I've found a lost part of myself. Blessed maybe, like the salesclerk said. Shiner puts us back onto the highway, headed east. To nowhere in particular. The road to nowhere goes in all directions.

I catch a glimpse of myself in the Buddy glasses in the passenger mirror. I don't hardly recognize myself. But I think, that's okay. I'm between things and it'll all be clear soon enough. We'll somehow not crash and burn, like Buddy. Or my folks.

We're well outside of Lubbock now, the brown west Texas landscape seeming to go on forever alongside the road to nowhere. But I have faith growing inside me. A tiny seed.

I sing, "If you knew Peggy Sue, you'd know why I feel blue."

Shiner nods but doesn't say anything. He looks calm – for now. It's hard for me to believe sometimes that he's ever killed anyone at all.

I look out at the dry land.

"Oh, Peggy, my Peggy Sue."

NOEL

At a gas station outside Dallas, I tell Shiner I need to know something. He's pumping gas and staring into the tank spout. I know to be patient and wait. I check the sky: it's dusk and streaks of red light fly away to the west.

"What is it, boy?"

He calls me a boy a lot. And numbnuts. I know that numbnuts means true irritation. Boy is more – neutral.

"What's noel, Shiner?"

He screws the cap back on the tank and slips the gas nozzle back in the pump. He looks around before looking at me.

"Were you born in a barn, Hap?" he says.

Calling me by my name means he's okay with the conversation. I shrug.

"It has to do with Christmas, right?"

"It's a Christmas carol," he says. "A song. Like Silent Fucking Night."

"Why's it called noel?"

"Beats fuck out of me, boy. It just is."

As we drive into Dallas, I notice red, green, and yellow Christmas lights and even sparkling Christmas trees in windows of passing houses.

"I never really had a Christmas, Shiner."

He glances at me – not the usual cold blue steel eyes, but softer. Surprised eyes, I reckon.

"Not even when you lived with your old grandfolks?"

"They had a shitty little metal tree with, like, four ornaments on it."

After a couple more miles, he says. "Didn't they get you presents, boy?"

"Just bullshit presents. A sweater from Kmart one time. It was ugly and too big. It was just in a store box. No wrapping.

After another mile, he says, "And what do you want me to do about all this? Do I look like Santa Fucking Claus?"

"Well, we could have us a Christmas, Shiner."

"I'll get right on it," he says. "It's the top of my list."

"I'm serious."

"I'm sure you are, boy."

But he glances at me a few times and then gets off the highway and we cruise a subdivision of nice houses. Expensive ones with garages big enough to house three or four cars. The houses and even garages all have lots of holiday lights strung around shrubs and along roofs. It's almost like daylight in that subdivision with so much light. I'd never seen the like of it.

He picks a house where there's only the warm glow from a Christmas tree in the front window. Nobody's home and he jimmies a back door. We're standing in a huge living room and the glowing Christmas tree must be seven feet tall. Presents wrapped in red, blue, and yellow paper cluster at its base. Shiner finds a beer in the fridge and sits in a chair, watching me rummage around in the presents.

"But only one," he says.

"Just one? Seriously?"

He holds up one finger. I look carefully at the presents and pick a big one and shake it but can't tell what it might be.

"But why only one, Shiner? There's so many."

"We need to get back on the road, boy," he says after hesitating and looking unsure. He glances at the window, watching for sudden car lights. His danger radar is turned up to high, I reckon.

I circle the tree and look carefully. A present with a large red bow stands out and I choose that one. I don't know why. Just a gut feeling, I suppose. Like I'm guided by some unseen force.

I'm holding the present on my lap, unopened, as we speed away and slip back on the highway, headed east into darkness.

Shiner glances at me.

"Well, boy – now you've had your Christmas."

"We'll see."

"Ain't you even going to open it, after all that trouble?"

"When it's Christmas."

"That's next week, Hap."

I clutch the present like it might fly away.

"I can wait."

"Yeah? Well, wait forever if you like. But that won't make that present yours, boy."

"It's mine now."

He laughs.

"Spoken like a true thief."

"You think so?"

I'm not sure how I feel about it.

"Maybe that's your true Christmas present," he says. "Knowing what you are."

I nod, but I'm pretty sure I don't know the answer to that yet.

THE BATES MOTEL

Shiner found us a cheap motel off the highway somewhere between Tyler, Texas and Shreveport, Louisiana. A crossroads in the middle of nowhere. We were "running on empty" for money, he said. I wasn't sure which state we were in. It was all the same to me. Endless nothing in any direction.

Borders was just a word.

The motel was shabby, smelly, the walls kind of greasy, if you ask me. There was a noisy heater rattling alongside the window. Shiner called it The Bates Motel.

"The sign says Moonlight Inn, Shiner. I can see it through the window."

He shakes his head and smirks.

"Don't you know nothing, boy?"

"Well, I can sure as shit read a flashing neon sign."

He pops the top of a Budweiser and has a big swig.

"The Bates Motel was in a famous movie, boy."

"Yeah? What's it called?"

"Psycho."

I nod and sip my beer. I don't know what to say for a while. I eat some more of the shitty pizza we got from a bar just down the road. I decide it's best to let the movie stuff go. Shiner sits on his bed and cleans his gun, a .44 magnum. A cannon. I've got a little .32 he gave me. I've only shot it once, at the house of that old couple up in Michigan. I wonder if Shiner knows whether I really did the deed or not. I know better than to tell him the truth. Maybe he knows and doesn't care. Maybe he didn't intend for me to do anything at all. Maybe it was just some fucked-up test. Maybe I thought I was taking the wrong test.

But I know I did the right thing for me.

Shiner stretches out and I turn on the TV low. He sleeps, that cannon beside him. Nothing on TV appeals to me. I go over to the window and sit there a while, watching the taillights of cars and trucks. The moon is pale and clouds drift across it.

A car pulls off the highway into the motel lot and its headlights are blinding for a moment. The car parks and I see a man, woman, and little child get out. They go into their room, and I can see them through their window, taking off their coats. The man hugs the woman and picks up his child, a girl. She clutches his neck while the woman has her arm around the man's waist.

Christmas was just a few days away and we were flat broke. Shiner would think up a score. Maybe as soon as Shreveport, if that was where we were headed. We had gas for a while. He cleaned his gun because he knew it was time to "go back to work."

I decided to clean mine, too, before getting some sleep. And I kept it next to me, too, just like him. But I couldn't sleep. I tossed and turned and finally sat up and watched the moon through the window a while. I glanced at Shiner, sound asleep, his cannon next to him like a favorite pet. A dog, maybe. He's not the cat type.

I know Shiner's killed. My gut says he killed that boy back in the MacDonald's lot and without hesitation or remorse. I suspect killing is easy for him. The war gave him that. There's a lot I don't know yet. I think of that movie he mentioned – Psycho. That's a word folks toss around a lot. It means all sorts of things. I believe I know what it means about Shiner. What that means for me.

Shiner turns over, facing me, still asleep, and his hand falls across his cannon. I pick mine up. I heft it in my hand and watch him sleep, hearing him breathe slowly. Once, I even aim it at him, but my hand shook, and I slowly put it down and sighed. That's not who I am.

That's good to know.

I finally sleep.

PASSING THROUGH SHREVEPORT

We're in a redneck bar outside Shreveport, drinking up the last of our cash. We can't even afford another round. Shiner sips his whiskey slowly and I nurse my beer. A plan would be welcome about now.

Shiner quietly tells me the song on the jukebox is Patsy Cline, who I don't know. She's feeling lonely and blue, the song says. I ask about her, but he merely shrugs and tosses the rest of his whiskey down. Miss Cline sings something to do with being crazy, as best as I can tell. But I can relate to crazy.

Shiner doesn't have a plan. He's uneasy and fidgets. The bartender, an enormous bald man with a walrus mustache, eyes Shiner like he knows exactly what sort he is. He maybe senses that Shiner is trouble. That makes Shiner even more nervous. It all might come to a head right there at the bar.

Shiner glances around, measuring distances, noting obstacles. Doors and such. I've seen the look before. I'm thinking this bar is not the place for trouble. I'd bet money we don't have that the bartender has a gun close by, maybe a shotgun just under the bar. In movies, that's usually where it is.

"There's a drug dealer here," I whisper to Shiner after the bartender moves down to a new customer.

Shiner nods and sips his whiskey.

"How do you know he's a dealer, numbnuts?"

"I heard him talking on a phone in the bathroom."

"Where is he?"

"Skinny dude in the John Deere cap. The booth by the door."

Shiner slowly swivels around and sizes the guy up. He gets that cold blue eyes stare I know so well. It means he's finally got a plan.

"Go tell him you want to buy. But outside. It has to be outside, boy."

I hesitate and finish my beer.

"Go on, now, boy."

Something occurs to me. Like maybe I'm crossing a bridge over a raging river. I'm in the middle of it, but not sure which side I should be on. Then I remember we're dead broke and nearly out of gas and my feet take over and I'm outside with this dealer, between a couple pickups. The dealer's face is half-lit by the moon. Suddenly, he stares at me, surprised, and I hear Shiner tell him to put his hands up.

"Motherfucker," the dealer hisses.

Shiner pivots and searches the dealer's pockets and finds the wad of cash. I can see Shiner's gun barrel against the dealer's head. Shiner cocks his gun. My pulse races.

"No," I said.

I can't quite see Shiner's face, but I know he's staring at me. I feel like I'm talking to a wolf trying to decide whether to lunge.

"We got what we want," I say. "Can't we just leave it at that?"

I hear the pleading in my voice.

Headlights from a car shine on us for a moment and I see Shiner's finger tight on the trigger. He glances at me, his face sort of twisted. I don't think it looks like him, not like when her hears some old song he remembers and liked once. He looks more like a wild animal than human. The thing that sometimes comes over him, the monkey on his back from Afghanistan, has its spurs in him again.

More headlights wash over us. I can see his eyes blinking fast. He coughs and it's like the car lights pierced him and manage to break the spell, the fever that took hold. Shiner slowly uncocks his gun and I'm able to exhale.

But Shiner still has a grip on the dealer and suddenly there's a moment where I think it could all just go to shit again and Shiner loses what little control he got back and wastes the poor dumb bastard. The dealer sobs and waits for the bullet, kind of hunched over, Shiner holding him by the neck from behind.

More car lights wash over us. I quietly tell Shiner it's time to go. Too many people. Too much light. Shiner finally nods and releases the guy. We push him in the truck and let him out a few miles down the road. Until that moment, I still half expected Shiner to shoot him.

"He'll have some story to tell," Shiner says, still sounding keyed-up.

"Yeah – to the cops."

"He's just a dickhead dealer, Hap. A cockroach that don't want any daylight."

"A cockroach that got robbed."

"He won't say nothing. He can't. His walk in the moonlight is the cost of doing business. That's all.

"If you say so."

But I had to admit it made sense.

After a while, he glances at me as we pass through Shreveport.

"How much did we get?"

"A few hundred."

"Fuck," Shiner says. "That's all? I reckon he was small-time."

"What are we?"

But Shiner doesn't answer.

REDNECK

It's Christmas Day and we're holed up in yet another seedy motel with a noisy heater. Just outside Birmingham, Alabama. We won't see much of Birmingham because we'll pull up stakes early in the morning and hit the road again. We're already low on cash and need a score. That's Shiner's department, figuring the score, and I leave him to it. Above my pay grade, Shiner tells me.

But now I know I must watch him closer than before. He damn near wasted that pissant drug dealer we robbed back in Shreveport. That was one close motherfucker of a call. In the moonlight, I could see Shiner's finger pressing the trigger. That dealer's brains were about to be splattered all over my shirt. That thing Shiner can't always shake from Afghanistan was spurring him on, and I managed to somehow talk him down.

Maybe that's why I'm along for the ride. At first, it was just to have steady meals. A dry place to sleep. But maybe now maybe I have a purpose. I like the notion of purpose. I never really had one. Didn't really know what one might look like until Shiner came along and plucked me off the streets.

My only purpose had been to not starve and not get fucked over by some pervert. And to not die from all the dumb ways homeless folks die, like neglect and loneliness. From just wearing out after a while.

"Another town, another redneck pizza," I say to Shiner.

The pepperoni's stale, the cheese watery, but I choke it down because at least it's filling. A trick learned from the streets. Eat when you can and what you can.

"This is Alabama, numbnuts," he says, smirking. "Everything they got here is redneck. Even the pizza."

"Can pizza really be redneck?"

He looks at the window, but from where he's sitting, he can't really see anything. Maybe some of the sky, which has been cloudy and gray all day.

"Sure it can," he says, nodding. "If it ain't for shit, then it's redneck."

He grins slightly, like he's proud of sounding clever, something I've never known him to care about.

"Well, it ain't that deep dish we had in Chicago," I said.

"And Birmingham ain't fucking Chicago by a longshot," he says, his voice rising. "But it's where we're at, boy."

"It ain't even the roast beef and mashed potatoes we had that first day we met, either."

"You want roast beef and potatoes?"

"I wouldn't say no."

"Well, then go buy some."

I pop open a Budweiser and hand Shiner one, too.

"How much cash we got left, Shiner?"

He shrugs and sips his beer.

"Not enough to make Chicago."

"That's some town alright."

"As good as it gets, I reckon."

"What about New York?"

"Fuck New York."

"You been there?"

"Too many times."

"So, we headed back there – Chicago?"

"It's damn cold up there right now," he says. "Be careful what you wish for."

"Well, it's not so hot here, either. I thought the south was always warm."

I see the first streaks from rain pouring down the window.

"I don't control the weather, boy."

Control's a funny deal. Folks like Shiner and me don't get to control much. We're the scavenger class, I reckon. Bottom feeders sucking up the scraps. Scores and drifting are what we control.

But somedays I think we're kidding ourselves that it's control. I think Shiner, what he does, is some sort of animal instinct.

He's a wolf among sheep people. Afghanistan gave him that. Fried him in it. He's only ever said enough about the war that I know it messed with his mind. It has its hooks in him. I think I must somehow keep the wolf on a leash so this gravy train can keep rolling.

"What about Florida, Shiner?"

He just shrugs and sips beer. He gets a stony look and keeps glancing at the window.

"What about it?"

"It's warmer there," I said. "And I've never been."

"You've seen one fucking palm tree, you've seen them all."

"I've never even seen one."

"Too many tourists in Florida."

"But, don't tourists have money? We don't."

He stares at me between sips of beer. I can't quite read his stone face. Then a rare smile plays along his lips. It's so rare that I think it makes him suddenly seem younger.

"Well, boy – you ain't as dumb as you look after all."

"You figure there's plenty of scores in Florida, Shiner?"

"Rich northern tourists," he says. "Easy marks. No more penny ante redneck drug dealers."

"So, fuck it," I said. "Let's just go now."

He hesitates. But I don't want to be penned up in this motel room in case something is trying to catch up to us. Always keep moving.

"Okay," he says, pulling what few clothes he has together. "By God, there's nothing stopping us."

I glance at the window, hoping that really is true. Once again, we're off into the unknown, on this road to nowhere we've been traveling.

Maybe the pizza's better in Florida.

DOUBLOONS

We drove all the way to Miami to finally find warmer temperatures. Some sort of cold front was sitting on the rest of Florida and rain fell everywhere. But it was dry and sunny in Miami and tourists in colorful clothes grazed in herds -- like sheep. Sheep to be sheared, Shiner said. The good weather and potential for scores had perked him up some.

We watched colorful tourists from a table outside a beachside bar. We were almost broke but managed a couple beers with something left for gas and a McDonald's run. I had no idea where we might sleep. Maybe in the truck. Down to the nub, was what Shiner liked to call it.

"We ought to dress like everybody else," I said, noticing all the Hawaiian shirts, shorts, flip-flops, and halter tops. We were like dark wolves creeping around the edges of a herd of bright sheep and I knew we stood out in dirty Levi's and wrinkled white t-shirts. The server, a young blond girl with a swishing ponytail, gave us the old evil eye. We didn't belong.

"You got any cash I don't know about?" Shiner said. "Not that I'm suggesting you might be a liar or anything."

"That's mighty good of you."

He smirked.

There was a twenty in my shoe. I'd kept it there since day one on the road to nowhere. I tossed it on the table and looked away.

"You been holding out on me, numbnuts?"

"It's just twenty bucks. Emergency food money, I reckon."

"You reckon, do you?"

"Next round's on me."

"You think so, boy? When were you going to say you had a twenty?"

I fidgeted in my seat.

"When it was time," I said. "Now I reckon it's time."

"I reckon so. We're down to the nub, boy."

"So you like to say."

He caught the whiff of attitude and cocked his head to a side.

"What's in your other shoe, boy? Fort Knox?"

"My foot. A sock. Toes."

"No silver bars or doubloons, funny boy?"

"What's a fucking doubloon?"

"Pirate coins – gold."

"I'll take another look. Maybe there's some doubloons rattling around down there."

"You're getting quite the mouth on you, numbnuts.

I leaned forward, elbows on the table.

"Maybe it's time to quit calling me numbnuts. Okay? Maybe it was funny and cute for a while. But now – it just sounds stupid."

Shiner's eyebrows arched but before he could speak, the server appeared, and I ordered a round of beers. I pushed the twenty toward her and she nodded like maybe we weren't so bad after all.

"And keep the change," I said.

"You got it, honey," she said, winking.

Shiner gazed out at the ocean for a moment and then at me, sharply.

"Well, boy – there went the old emergency food fund."

I didn't care to be called boy, but after we'd just retired numbnuts, I figured dumping boy was a good next project. Everything in good time.

"I reckon you'll just have to figure out something, Shiner. Ain't you the brains of this outfit?"

He leaned back against his chair and glanced around at tourists jamming the beach and bar.

"We need us some of them gold doubloons," he said.

"Tell me something I don't know."

He shot me a look but didn't say anything. Maybe he'd accepted my newfound attitude. Or the other shoe would still fall. With Shiner, it could be a crapshoot.

"Let's go," he said abruptly. I hadn't finished my beer, but I knew to just go without asking why. I figured he was on to something, and I followed him past several tables downstairs to the street. After we crossed and stood under a towering palm tree, he showed me the smart phone he'd lifted.

"So, now you've got a cell phone," I said, not impressed.

"Not just a cell phone, boy. A smart phone."

"So?"

I really didn't know shit about cell phones.

"We can pawn it for a couple hundred," he said, grinning.

"We need more than that."

"I know. But this gets us off the street and on real beds tonight, boy."

I nodded.

"Okay -- that works."

"Now we find a pawn shop."

"What's the plan after that?"

"One thing at a time, boy."

I stopped walking. Shiner turned back to me, flashy tourists cruising all around us.

"What's this bullshit?" he said.

"No more boy this and boy that, Shiner. We clear on that?"

He nodded as people brushed by us.

"I'll follow you, Shiner. But as Hap. Only as Hap. No more names."

"Okay, Hap. Deal." We shook hands and he handed me the phone. "You can even do the damn talking at the pawn store."

I swallowed hard.

That was the other shoe dropping.

PELICANS

We stole enough smart phones in Miami bars and restaurants to raise a couple grand from pawn shops. Righteous bucks after all the penny ante bullshit we'd pulled robbing small time drug dealers on our way south. Shiner was careful to just sell one phone per store. It took all day to raise the cash. But Shiner said it was the numbnuts who tried to land a whale all at once who got caught.

Shiner got us a decent motel room up the coast a good distance from Miami, up around Boca Raton. The Sea Ray Palms Motel. Good AC in the room. It smelled good, too – fresh. Sea fresh, the motel advertised. Walking distance to the beach. Don't eat where you shit, was what Shiner said about putting Miami in the rearview mirror for now.

There was a seafood joint across the road from the motel and we could see the beach from there. It wasn't a fancy place and we fit in okay after buying touristy T-shirts at a store next to the motel. My shirt had a large pelican on the front. I'd never seen a pelican. Its long beak struck me as amazing.

"Pelicans," Shiner said quietly, like it was an old stale joke he was tired of hearing.

"What about them, Shiner? I've never seen one."

He looked at the beach and pointed to docks beyond.

"You'd likely find some over at the docks," he said. "Rooting about for food."

"They can swim?"

"What? Of course they can swim."

"And they can fly?"

"Yeah, they can fucking fly. I swear, Hap, sometimes you sound like you were born in a barn."

"I really don't know what that means."

"Well, trust me – it fits."

"If you fucking say so."

"I fucking do, but, whatever."

We drank a couple beers. The sun was warm on my forehead. It was the most relaxed we'd been in weeks. We had money. A decent place to sleep and good food. But there was a time limit to it. We'd have to get back to work soon and find some scores. Shiner said we'd might as well take a few days and live in the tall cotton. Be tourists and all that.

"Don't you like pelicans, Shiner?"

He shrugged and ordered us more beers from the skinny blond server.

"I like 'em just fine, I reckon. I just don't want to hear about them all the damn time is all."

"I only mentioned them the one time."

He sipped his beer and looked at the ocean a while. I knew he was mulling something. Maybe when and how we'd score next. I was already back to thinking about pelicans.

He suddenly said, "My momma used to talk about pelicans. She'd never seen one, either. She died without ever seeing a pelican."

"Why'd she talk about them?"

"She was a religious woman."

He looked off again at the water but maybe seeing his mother, I figured.

"What's that got to do with pelicans, Shiner?'

"She said they were symbols -- Christ sacrificing himself for mankind." He shook his head and smirked. "What did all that sacrifice get us, I wonder."

"We're doing okay, ain't we?"

Shiner's face sort of darkened, despite the bright sunlight. He glanced at the ocean. There were a few clouds forming far off.

"Maybe just pure dumb luck, Hap. No magic to it at all."

"Well, you know your business," I said. "Maybe it's skill."

He managed a thin smile.

"Maybe." He looked again at the water. "You just keep thinking that, Hap. Believe in magic. Right up to judgment day."

"What day is that?"

"Maybe sooner than we think. How about them apples?"

"I don't like apples."

"Well, there you go."

We walked down the beach over to some docks, but Shiner stayed back when I walked out on them.

"You go ahead, Hap. I've done seen all the pelicans I need to see. Go find some magic if that floats your boat."

I walked past fancy boats of all sizes, people on them sipping mixed drinks and looking me over as I went by. I figured they didn't think I belonged. Rich fucks, Shiner called them. I sat on a dock for a while and sure enough, a pelican sailed by. It cruised over to me, but I didn't have anything for it and so it just went on, around the stern of a boat.

I waited to feel some magic, but there wasn't any.

BIRTHDAY

We've been at the Sea Ray Palms Motel now for a few days and that's longer than me and Shiner have stayed anywhere in months. We get coffee and donuts in a diner every morning, just across the street from the Sea Ray. Just like regular folks not selling stolen smart phones.

From a diner window we can see the beach and chatty gulls circling tourists. I like to watch tankers or freighters cruise offshore while I munch my donuts and Shiner dips his in coffee.

"But this ain't home, Hap," Shiner says, dipping a donut. "Don't get that notion lodged in your head."

"How much money we got?"

"Enough. For now."

The servers know us now at this diner. Shiner tips generously. They wink at us, but mostly they're older ladies. In their forties, I reckon. Or fifties. I guess that's old to me. It gets me thinking and I glance at a calendar on the wall: today is my birthday.

I'm eighteen now. Growing up in foster homes I ditched first chance I got, birthdays were not a deal. Never celebrated. No cake and Cokes and presents. Just another day. But now I'm eighteen. I think that means something. I just don't know what.

Am I a man now? What with all the thieving I've done with Shiner, it seems like that's been fact a while. Before Shiner, on the streets, I grew up fast. It was sink or swim. I was dogpaddling when Shiner took me in.

"Today?" Shiner says. "For real, boy? Your fucking birthday?"

"You said you wouldn't call me boy. Now I'm eighteen and that don't work at all."

He nods and glances at the ocean.

"I reckon you're right, Hap. My bad."

I think I do feel different somehow. But I'm not sure just how.

"I need to have me a real birthday, Shiner."

"Why's that?"

"Because I never had one."

"Uh-huh," he says, dipping a donut. "And what's that look like – a real birthday?"

I look at waves breaking on the beach. A tanker chugs along offshore and its bow wave is foamy white and clean – fresh. That tanker is probably headed far off. Someplace exotic, like maybe

Venezuela. I can't even imagine what Venezuela might be like. Our Sea Ray room with fresh sheets and a piney scent in the air every morning is as exotic as I've seen.

"I reckon I need a girl." Then I remember I'm eighteen now. "A woman, I mean."

"Don't we all?" he says. He's dunking another donut in his coffee. Then he looks up sharply. "Wait -- you telling me you ain't never done the dirty deed?"

I shake my head.

"I think I'd remember if I did."

"Not even with them young gals on the streets?"

"They smelled bad, Shiner."

"You're kind of picky, eh?"

"And they didn't brush their teeth."

"Well, beggars can't be choosers, Hap," he says, chuckling, but then he sees I'm serious. One of the older servers comes by and tops off our coffees.

"What about her?" Shiner says when she's gone. He grins.

"For you, maybe."

His eyes narrow.

"I ain't that old yet, boy."

"Hap."

"Okay – Hap," he says. "Hap, the eighteen-year-old man."

"Don't fuck with me, Shiner."

"Believe me, son – I ain't the one who'd be fucking with you."

"Don't call me son, either."

He laughs but I give him a cold stare.

"Okay – Hap. But listen, that's a tall order you're asking. Back in Detroit, I'd know where to go. Here, it'll take some recon to figure out."

"We've got enough money?"

"If we cut our stay at the Sea Ray shorter – yeah, we have enough."

"I'll miss the Sea Ray."

"Look at it this way – you can enjoy fresh motel sheets or dirty up some sheets and get your cherry popped good and proper."

"Why's it called a cherry? I never got that."

Shiner waved the server back for more coffee.

"You got any fresh pie?"

"Verna made cherry pie this morning," she said.

"Perfect," Shiner said. "How about a slice for my friend here. It's his birthday."

"Happy birthday," she said. "How old are you?"

"Eighteen."

I tried to smile politely.

"Do you like cherry pie?" she asked.

"I reckon we're going to find out," I said, looking over Shiner's shoulder at a tanker offshore.

Its bow wave flowed fast and high.

MERRY-GO-ROUND

Shiner said Jacksonville was where to go to get my cherry popped. He got that news from a guy in a bar just down from where we stayed at The Sea Ray Palms Motel.

"Was this guy drunk?"

"What fucking difference does that make, Hap?"

"Maybe he was fucking with you about Jacksonville."

"Why would he do that?"

"Because he was drunk?"

"Information is information, drunk or sober. Drunk's when people are most honest, boy."

"No more boy – remember? We have an understanding. I'm eighteen now."

"I stand corrected – Hap."

"Okay. But Jacksonville's way the hell up north. Miami is just down the road from here. Seems like Miami is better for what I want."

"Miami is where we swipe smart phones and sell them – in case you forgot what paid for a clean motel for a change."

We were at the diner across from the motel. Shiner dunked his donut in coffee. I tried it once, but it didn't take.

"Seems like you're just watering down a perfectly good donut. And the sugar gets washed off."

"Well, it's my fucking donut, Hap. And my sugar."

"Pardon me for living."

"Besides, the sugar drips into the coffee. It all goes to the same place."

I looked out a window at the ocean, but there were no tankers or freighters cruising with streaming bow waves. Maybe the ships were farther out. One of the servers said a big storm was brewing offshore. Mega-rain coming, she said.

"A storm's no good for us," Shiner said, dunking a donut. "If we want to go to work again in Miami, that is. Jacksonville's way the fuck north. No storms up there, I reckon."

"And we've never worked Jacksonville," I said.

"There's that, too. You're learning –"

"Hap," I said quickly. "You're learning – Hap."

"That's what I was going to say."

"Uh-huh."

"You know, you're getting to be kind of a contrary sonofabitch, Hap."

"I'm eighteen now – I'm a man."

Shiner smirked and wiped his mouth with a napkin.

"Well, there's more to it than turning eighteen – Hap."

"Like what?"

"Lots of things."

"What things? Like going to Afghanistan? Is that where you learned to be a man?"

Shiner never wanted to talk about Afghanistan. But I figured if now I'm a man and can be contrary, then asking goes with the territory. A new privilege. He gave me a glance but there wasn't much heat behind it, like when I'd asked before and he'd just shut me down and tell me it was none of my fucking pissant business.

"Don't bark up the wrong tree, Hap."

But he said it calmly. He grinned at the server when she topped off his coffee. Our days at The Sea Ray Palms Motel with clean sheets and pine scent in the air had relaxed him some, his Afghanistan demons banished for now. I knew it was maybe up to me to keep them that way, but I feared I was not up to the job. I'd managed to talk him down from pulling the trigger on that drug dealer back in Shreveport. But maybe that was just dumb fucking luck.

"Do we really need guns to steal smart phones?"

Shiner frowned and looked around quickly to see where the servers were.

"Keep that shit under your hat in public – Hap."

"Well – do we?"

"A gun's a good thing to have when you need one."

"Like back in Michigan, where them old folks lived?"

"Don't dig that back up, boy."

I gave him a pass on calling me boy. I figured he was entitled to it one more time. We were in the ditch now and it would be interesting to see how we got out.

"I didn't shoot them," I said.

He looked around but the servers huddled at the register gabbing about weather.

"I didn't think you did -- Hap."

"But you told me to."

"And you made your choice when I left the house."

"It was just some fucked up test?"

He sighed and stared in his coffee a moment.

"You want to know what it means to be a man?" he said, looking up sharply. "It means knowing what's right for you and not giving a fuck what's right for others."

The server came over and topped his coffee. Shiner smiled politely.

I suppose Shiner meant to offer some kind of wisdom, but I took it only as a confession he'd kill again one day, when the demons gripped him. I didn't yet know how I'd jump off this crazy merry-go-round.

But I knew I needed to start looking for the exit.

KUMBAYA

For the first time since we'd hit the road to nowhere, me and Shiner had a cash reserve. A cash cushion, he called it when he patted the wad of bills in his jeans pocket. Those smart phones we'd lifted down in Miami had set us up okay and now we stayed in a good motel near the beach, just north of Jacksonville in St. Augustine.

Shiner said it was wise to stay outside Jacksonville, where we'd soon resume our smart phone pilfering. That was his word for it, pilfering. I'd never heard that before. He would laugh and say pilfering made what we did sound less like a crime and more like a profession.

Like we'd agreed to down in Miami, some of the cash cushion would go to popping my cherry once he'd located where to do that in Jacksonville. I tried not thinking about being a virgin, which is an odd thing nowadays for an eighteen-year-old man-boy to be, but it was hard because I thought of first-time sex as like waiting for a raging warm river to jump its banks and pull you under and spit you out on the other side.

Of what?

I had no idea.

I'd seen porn films and sex looked messy, sweaty, and gymnastic, bodies flopping about like a fish on a dock, and it sure seemed like porn ladies mentioned God a lot. The men grunted, breathed hard, and made faces, and I wondered if that was how I'd be with the hooker Shiner drummed up. It seemed to lack – dignity. But, up to this point, my life hadn't been exactly dignified, and the prospects didn't seem all that promising. We weren't really living beyond day to day.

But the sex thing got me thinking about when we visited that Buddy Holly place in Texas, where I heard how Mr. Holly stuttered-like when he sang about Peggy Sue. Shiner told me hookers don't give real names – like Peggy Sue. They cook up exotic ones, like Dominique or Veronique. I figured when it was time, I'd think of her as Peggy Sue. I might even sing the song in my head while I did the dirty deed..

"Why's sex dirty, Shiner?"

"Man, you really were born in a barn," he said, shaking his head.

"I still don't know what that means. And you say it all the time."

"Think about it."

I shrugged.

"I got no clue. I've never even been in a barn. I was born in the air, on a plane over Ohio."

"So you've said. Fifty times."

"Well, it's true."

"I'm not calling you a liar, Hap."

"Well, you'd be wrong if you did." After a moment, I said, "When was your first time, Shiner?"

"Jesus," he said. "Men don't sit around talking about shit like that, Hap. That's what women do."

"Why can't we talk about it?"

"Well, for starters, this ain't some Kumbaya moment were having here, you know."

"I don't know what that is – Kumbaya."

"It don't matter."

"Then why say it at all?"

He frowned.

"Okay, Hap. Fine. If you really need to know -- my mother sang that song sometimes. Kumbaya is a song."

"What kind of song?"

"It's religious. So was she. But I've told you that before."

"What's the song about?"

He smiled and then chuckled, clearly tickled about something.

"Well, I really only remember one line from it."

"Yeah? What line's that?"

"Arise and come."

Then he laughed loudly.

"What's so damn funny?"

He looked at me and slowly smirked.

"Don't you get it? That's going to be you, Hap."

"What do you mean?"

"When I find you a hooker and get your damn cherry busted, you'll arise, and then you'll come – Kumbaya, motherfucker."

He kept laughing.

"Fuck-you," I said and left the motel.

I walked over to the beach, where there was a nice breeze. Waves crashed on the sand. Some geezer hunched over a metal detector was the only person on the beach. White gulls hovered above me, chatting as if they knew some secret and were willing to let me in on it. I was willing to listen.

After a while, I kicked off my shoes and socks and let the water wash over my toes. And then my ankles. It felt surprisingly warm. Soothing. Then I waded on up to my knees. And then over my thighs. I thought, this is how everything new in life begins, just a little bit at a time, and you shouldn't rush it.

MIRACLE MAGIC VAGINA

Shiner let her in and was out the door before the hooker had unslung her white purse. She glanced around with dark eyes shaded by thick eyelashes. I sensed that those searchlight eyes didn't miss much. I reckon she knew to size things up.

Hooker 101.

Me and Shiner were that way, too, every time we set out to swipe smart phones in public places. Working under the main tent, Shiner called it, with an audience. You never knew for sure what you'd walked into. Where the exit was. I supposed knowing the exit was Hooker 101, too. I figured me and that hooker were like colleagues working different parts of a big store.

"So," she said, drawing the word out and shifting her weight to one leg. "Bill tells me this is your first time, Tony."

She smiled and it made her suddenly go from ordinary to pretty.

"Tony?"

Her head cocked sharply to a side, and she glanced back at the door, measuring the distance, I supposed. More Hooker 101. Be ready for anything.

"Oh, right," I said, grinning. "Tony. Or Anthony. I'm good both ways."

She smirked.

"You ain't really a Tony or an Anthony," she said.

"Does it matter?"

She took one more look around, glancing again at the door. She seemed like a cat that could hear the slightest sound far off in a corner.

"No, Hun – it don't matter much. This ain't a real names kind of business. But I'll call you Tony, or Herbert – or Daffy Duck. Whatever, if it gives your friend a rise."

"Hun works okay, I reckon."

I smiled and so did she and the tension eased.

I didn't know how to start and so I just waited with a big dumb grin on my face, and she took over and I was out of my clothes with little sense of how they came off and then we were at it, her guiding my thrusting hips with surprisingly strong hands gripping my waist.

Time seemed to slow down to like a slow-motion scene in a movie. I know it wasn't a long time. It was as if there was no world outside the middle of the bed and our scents mixing with sweat. It was – miraculous. It was a sensation like none I'd ever known. It was like – like searching frantically along a street and finding the right house, warm and glowing, and knowing you'd finally come home.

And then I did come, abruptly, and she smiled that sweet smile again. For a moment that I couldn't measure with time, I felt like we had melted into each other, the liquid connection like two rivers colliding and absorbing each other, spilling over their banks.

It was a kind of magic I'd never imagined. After we'd dressed, she accepted a beer and sat in a chair. I was still glowing, the magic coursing throughout me.

"For real?" she said. "That was your first time?"

I nodded and sipped beer. A glow percolated throughout me. It was physical, but also mental. An attitude? Maybe a new way of seeing the world. I doubted I could explain it. I sure didn't feel like a kid anymore. The miracle vagina changed that for good.

"It was – awesome."

She smiled the same practiced smile a cashier flashes to each customer at a supermarket. And then I couldn't make eye contact. I wanted to ask her real name, but there was no point to that. It would just be a word. She would not give it, the true name. Maybe that was the last privacy she could protect in a business that lacked it altogether. I knew better than to tell her my name. I was learning the ropes about living in the shadows.

She finished her beer and stood up.

"You want some advice – Tony?"

"Always."

"Ditch your partner – Bill," she said, slinging her purse over her shoulder. "Or whatever his fucking name is."

I nodded but had to ask.

"Why's that?"

"I know his type, Hun. Seen a few of him before."

"What's his type?"

"He ain't on a two-way street. It's all one way. No stop signs. And it won't turn out well."

"He was in Afghanistan," I said weakly.

She nodded, getting it.

"He still is, Hun. But you don't have to be."

She lit a cigarette at the door and exhaled blue smoke.

"My name's Hap," I said, for no other reason than I could.

"Hap," she said, assessing it. "That short for anything?"

"Not really."

"Hap's a good name." She opened the door and stood in the doorway a moment, looking back at me. "But get out from under Mr. Bill, Hap, before he kills you."

She winked and was gone as the magic faded.

EXPENDABLE

The first phones we swiped in Jacksonville weren't smart phones and that pissed off Shiner royally. We even accidentally netted a flip phone as we left some dive bar after a burger break. Shiner tossed it against a brick wall in the alley.

"What's wrong with these Jacksonville clucks -- can't they afford a fucking smart phone?"

"I reckon it's because not everybody's rich," I said lamely.

"Fuck that," Shiner said. "And you know what this means, don't you, Hap? It means we didn't even get lunch and the brewskis covered. That came out of our own pockets."

"So, next time we'll hit the motherlode, for sure."

He looked amused.

"You even know what that means, Hap—motherlode?"

"Not really. But I know it's a good thing. I remember you said so a few times back in Miami."

"That was Miami. A better class of people to steal from. More money down there."

"We just have to find the right places up here, don't you reckon?"

"Uh-huh," Shiner said, managing to dial his anger back a notch. We walked down the street. He looked back at the bar. "My bad, Hapster. That piss hole wasn't smart phone territory. I should have known it."

"Now you're calling me Hapster?"

He grinned and smacked my back. A little too hard.

"Shit, bro – you have to admit it beats hell out of when I always called you numbnuts."

"And boy. Don't forget boy."

"You ain't no boy no more, Hapster."

"Reckon not."

"You're eighteen now and got your ashes hauled good and proper by a hooker who knew her business."

I nodded but avoided eye contact.

"She did okay by you, Hapster? Popped your cherry just right?"

"Men don't talk about sex, Shiner. You told me that."

He shook his head.

"You're misremembering, Hapster. I said men don't talk about sex with wives or girlfriends. But hookers are different. That's fair game."

"Why's that?"

"Because they're just whores."

I thought back to when the hooker popped my cherry two nights back. She was nice, gentle. When she smiled, her face lit up. She didn't make sex seem sleazy. More like a very useful lesson. Like renting a tutor.

"Where'd you find her, Shiner?"

"In a bar. But don't worry, Hapster – I tried her first. Wouldn't want to palm bad goods off on you."

"Mighty kind of you," I said, trying to wish away the image of him with her first. I don't think he got the sarcasm.

"I look out for you, Hapster. You know that."

"Do I?"

That sort of just popped out quick and he glared at me. That glare I'd seen from time to time, the cold blue eyes stare when you could almost feel the heat behind it. I realized the hooker had seen that stare and felt that heat, too. That's why she warned me to get out before Shiner killed me because he would eventually. She'd done business with his type before.

I think standing there that day on a sidewalk, as Shiner's mind shifted back to hunting smart phones, I finally understood it was just a matter of time before I no longer served whatever purpose he saw in me, and I became expendable. I could just leave, but I had nowhere to go, no skills to make a living. Shiner held the money, the take, when we fenced phones in pawn shops. He only gave me pocket money. That was control.

And that cut down the options. I could kill him before he did me, but I didn't know if that was even in me. I hoped to God it wasn't. Most days, I felt sure it wasn't. But when you're expendable, your life on the line, good and bad don't figure into it. When you're expendable, morals are for other people.

"Something on your mind, Hap?"

His eyes narrowed and there was some heat building behind the stare.

"Not a thing, Shiner."

"Uh-huh," he said. "But you'd say if there was?"

"You'll be the first to know. Guaranteed."

"Ain't no guarantees in life, Hap."

"Don't I know it."

His glare lingered and I kept my smile and tight eye contact. We were just a foot apart, like two boxers touching gloves and waiting for the first-round bell to sound. Then he nodded grudgingly, and we walked toward upscale downtown, where scoring phones might be better, him shooting me that creepy side glance to remind me he had eyes on me.

I smirked and rolled my eyes when he wasn't looking. I nodded when he glanced again. It felt like for the first time, we both understood each very well and that maybe he knew he couldn't trust me completely and he'd eventually be forced to make a decision about that.

I got the feeling that time was running out.

BEFORE THE WHIP COMES DOWN

I started holding out on Shiner. That was risky with his temper. Hell, he'd see it as treason. But I needed my own money and not just the odd twenty – sometimes even a fifty -- he floated me for walking around. I'd swipe a phone without him knowing, while he was at a pawn shop down in Jacksonville cashing in. There was a pawn shop here in St. Augustine, a long walk from the motel, and that was my secret ATM.

I knew it went against the rules, to do business where we lived – Shiner had drilled it into me that we "didn't shit where we ate." I knew it was Common Sense Survival 101. But I didn't see I had much choice. When you don't have options, rules are just words. Suggestions at most.

There was a cover story – a lie – I worked up in case he found out: It wasn't treason, I'd point out, because I'd claim I was practicing – sharpening my skills – and intended to surprise him once the money grew to a righteous amount. I felt it sounded okay, that he might go for it. I even practiced saying it when I walked along the beach with noisy gulls trailing me. I scored several smart phones in bars down there.

But one day Shiner announced that the smart phone market was drying up in Jacksonville. Just like that, risk had gone up. The pawn people told him the police had eyes on things, had come sniffing around. We'd done our work too well, he said, smirking, and now it was time to beat feet "before the whip comes down."

"What's that from?"

"A song, Hapster. The Rolling Stones. You do know who they are, don't you?"

"Yeah, sure. I've heard of them."

"Oh, you've heard of them, have you? Just heard of them?"

I nodded and knew to pretend interest in rock and roll, which I knew was maybe the one thing that interested Shiner beyond stealing and living on our road to nowhere.

"Is this going to be like when we went to that museum in Texas to learn about Buddy Holly?"

"No, Hap."

I heard the irritation in his voice.

"It ain't that at all," he said, now exasperated. "It's just a line from a fucking song."

Well, it's sort of catchy," I said. "That line."

"Fucking damn right it's catchy," Shiner said, his eyes bulging. But I figured most of that was because the smart phone market dried up. The whip had done come down on that.

"Okay, then," I said, and we packed our few things and hopped in the truck and drove north out of St. Augustine. After a few miles I said, "We headed anywhere in particular?"

He didn't say anything for a few more miles. I could tell he was stewing. Likely from having to beat feet out of Florida, which is where we'd stayed the longest, where we lived halfway decently and ate good and even had nice tans. That was where I got my cherry popped and I looked forward to another round of that once we got situated elsewhere.

The cost of another hooker, I reminded myself happily, would come out of our general fund, which Shiner regulated closely, and I wouldn't have to tap into my own secret fund. I was leaning the ropes of life on the road to nowhere. I felt a little better about hitting the road again because of the cash in my pocket.

"What's the next big town up this way?" I asked Shiner.

"Savannah."

"How far?"

"Just up the road a spell."

"Savannah, Florida," I said.

"No, Hap – Savannah ain't in Florida. It's in Georgia."

"Has it always been in Georgia?"

I don't think he caught on I was just fucking with him.

"Yeah, it always has. They haven't moved it or anything."

"Good to know."

"Maybe we need to buy you a fucking map so you can learn about your damn country."

"It ain't my country, Shiner. I was born in a plane in the air, over Ohio -- remember? I'm from the air."

"How could I forget. You told that story fifty times. But here's a news flash, Hapster – the air was over America and so you're still American."

"Maybe."

"Ain't no maybe about it."

After a while I said, "We got enough dough to stay okay in Savannah?"

"But we'll be back on a budget."

I thought, maybe you'll be on a budget, but I'll build my secret fund. A day of reckoning was coming. I could feel it. It hung in the air.

Maybe as soon as Savannah, the final whip would come down.

GRACELAND

But we didn't go to Savannah. We ditched Georgia altogether. Shiner got one of his wild rock and roll hairs up his ass and wheeled us north until we hit Memphis. I'd never been. I asked what was in Memphis, besides more smart phones we could steal and pawn, and he had his standard look of utter disgust at my ignorance.

"But don't say I was born in a barn, Shiner. We've done covered that ground."

"Right," he said, nodding and tapping the steering wheel. "You're the famous air boy, the dipshit born in a plane. Heard the tale, Hap. A million times."

"Let's add dipshit to the list of names we can retire," I said.

"It's getting to be a long list, Hapster."

"But I reckon we can keep Hapster."

"Really?"

"I sort of like it, actually."

"Then I'll just call you Hap."

He cackled and smacked the steering wheel hard.

"You're fucked up, Shiner. Totally."

"Ain't we all?"

"Some more than others."

He shot me his usual creepy side glance.

"But at least I fucking know who Elvis Presley was, dildo."

"Dildo goes on the banned list, too."

"Fuck you, Hap. Fuck your list."

"Okay, okay," I said. "Yeah, I know who he was -- supposedly the king of rock and roll."

"Supposedly? Seriously? There's only ever been but one king, Hapster — Elvis."

"But who made him king?"

Shiner glanced again, a look of surprise.

"What kind of dipshit question is that?"

"We retired dipshit."

"I'm reviving it, dipshit. The fans made him king—who else?"

I knew to quit while I was ahead. Or at least not running too far behind. When we reached Memphis, Shiner took us to Graceland right off. I was amazed by the big music notes and dueling guitar players on the iron gates to the house.

Shiner was amazed at the standard tour price.

"Fuck me, Jesus," he said. "That's near a couple hundred bucks. That chews a bite out of our cash reserve."

"Well, then maybe you'll just have to skip the King."

He glared.

"We coughed it up for your hooker back in Jacksonville. We can cough it up for the King."

I wasn't impressed. We didn't see all that much. A few rooms. I thought Elvis's living room looked like an old lady's. A lot of white furniture, white walls, white carpeting. It'd all be a bitch to keep clean. The tour guide said the décor was vintage 60s and 70s. I thought there was a funny odor to the place.

Shiner looked like he'd seen the second coming of Jesus. I guess to him, Elvis was sort of that, too. After the tour was over, Shiner was quiet. Reverent? Hard to say with him, but he even told me to drive for a change and look for a decent motel. Something on the outskirts of town. He seemed lost in thought. We ended up down south of the city, out by the highway for a quick getaway.

I turned on the room TV and watched a movie. It was Bonnie and Clyde. Shiner stretched out on his bed and stared at the ceiling, still in his Elvis fog, I figured. Bonnie and Clyde got shot up pretty damn good at the end. Shiner had to tell me who they were.

After a while, I said, "You figure that'll happen to us, Shiner?"

It took him a moment to turn his head my way.

"Fuck if I know," he finally said weakly.

"What do you suppose Elvis would say about it?"

"Thank you very much," he said, trying – badly -- to sound like Elvis. He explained the reference to me. Then he looked off, at a corner of the room.

"What does that mean, exactly?" I said.

"Hell, fuck if I know. I reckon it's just how folks remember Elvis."

Then he took his gun out of his bag and cleaned it, while I sat and looked at the wall, every now and then glancing at him as he worked on his gun.

RECRUITER

Memphis was a drag. Shiner sank into a funk for a few days. No reason for it that I could tell. Just – poof, his lights went out. Nobody's home. He stopped talking. We lived off delivered pizza and I only got sprung from the room to make a beer run with my fake ID. I killed time watching boring movies while he stared at the ceiling from bed. I'd never seen him like that. He got up once to clean his gun, even though he'd done it just two nights before.

I had half a notion to tiptoe out while he napped and take the truck and get off the road to nowhere we'd been on for months. But I didn't know where I'd go. I had money saved up, but no clue if it was enough to start over someplace. Doing what? I'd just tuned eighteen and hadn't even finished high school. Swiping smart phones to pawn wasn't much of a job skill to brag about. If I even had a resume, that'd be the only item on it.

Three days into Shiner's funk, I told him I was making a beer run and would hunt up better pizza than we'd had. Or maybe some Asian food – he liked Asian food. Or Mexican. None of that got a rise out of him. He just nodded weakly. The ceiling was now his best friend.

I could tell he was way down low because he'd never liked the idea of me just taking off in the truck. Now he just managed a "whatever" and went back to staring at the ceiling. He even handed over a wad of cash to me, much more than I'd need. It wasn't like him to be so casual with our dough. And he didn't bother to remind me to be careful driving in a stolen truck.

At first, I just drove around Memphis, mindful to obey signs and drive the limit and not arouse any suspicion. At a light, I looked over at a strip mall. There was an Army recruiting office there and without much thought, I turned in and went inside. A tall soldier with a shaved head and a crisp uniform and medals on his breast stood up from behind his desk as I entered. He smiled and swept his hand toward a chair. His hand was huge, like a catcher's mitt

"Have a seat, pardner. What's your name?"

"Billy."

That was the first thing that came to me. I'd just watched a movie about Billy the Kid.

"I'm Sgt. Brodsky," he said, offering his meaty hand across the desk and we shook. His grip was strong. My hand disappeared inside his.

"So, Billy," he said. "Thinking of serving your country?"

"I don't know."

I figured honesty was the way to go.

"That's okay," he said, nodding. "It's a big step, for sure."

Then he launched into a story about growing up on a farm in Nebraska and joining the Army and going to Afghanistan and how it made him the man he is today. My first thought was that Afghanistan made Shiner the man he is today, but he bore no resemblance to hearty Sgt. Brodsky.

"So," I said. "What happens when you come back from the war?"

He frowned.

"I'm not sure I understand, son."

"Well, when my uncle got back, he just stayed in bed a lot and stared at the ceiling."

Sgt. Brodsky looked down for a moment, at his clasped hands resting on the desk.

"Well, it takes time – to readjust."

He smiled bravely.

"My uncle has guns, Sgt. Brodsky. He takes them everywhere he goes. I had to stop him from shooting somebody one time."

Sgt. Brodsky looked alarmed.

"That man needs help."

"Tell me about it," I said.

"I'd be happy to meet with him, Billy."

"I don't know."

"What don't you know?"

"What to do."

But I knew I was talking more about me than Shiner.

"If you bring him here, maybe I can help him – brother to brother."

I didn't think Shiner would cotton up to Sgt. Brodsky as a brother.

"Okay. Maybe I'll try."

"What about you?" Sgt. Brodsky said.

"What about me?"

"The Army is a fine career for a young man such as yourself. And it will pay for college, too. Does that appeal to you, Billy?"

"I don't know."

He eased back in his chair. I abruptly got up and left and he didn't say a word. I sat in the truck for a moment. I could see Sgt. Brodsky shuffling papers at his desk. I started the truck and headed west toward the interstate north. But after a while I turned off and went back to the motel.

I don't know why.

That worried me.

LOOKED LIKE RAIN

Somehow, Shiner snapped out of it. There wasn't one thing I'd say did it. He just slid his legs off the motel bed, hesitated, and stood. Sort of wobbly, after days in bed. He'd been down and now he was up. I listened to him shower and when he came out, he tried a smile, but it was lopsided.

"Earth to Shiner," I said. "Establishing contact."

I'd heard that line in a sci-fi on the motel TV. I'd watched movies and made beer and pizza runs for days.

"Real fucking funny, Hap. Hilarious."

"You okay, man?"

"Why wouldn't I be?"

"Well, maybe 'cause you just spent days in bed staring at the ceiling."

"Maybe I like the ceiling. Maybe it's a pretty good ceiling."

I glanced up.

"It's white. Smooth. And white. Did I mention white? And smooth?"

"Well, it didn't give me no dipshit guff. How about that, Hap?"

I looked away.

"This got anything to do with when we went to Graceland, and you saw where the King did all his King shit?"

Shiner sat in a chair, hands gripping armrests like he expected it to just take off.

"You kids today don't appreciate style. And real music. Elvis could sing. He had style. That's why he was the King."

I grabbed two Buds from the cooler and handed him one. He took a long swig.

"What you got against rap, Shiner?"

"It ain't music. That's what. It's a mopey turd in a hoodie talking on a stage."

I knew to just let it go.

"We ain't worked since we got here," I said. "Think about how many smart phones are waiting to be lifted. Memphis probably has good pawn shops. There's one just down the street."

He sipped beer and scowled.

"Them phones are a dead end."

"We make some coin from them."

"Until we run out of pawn shops because cops sniff around."

"Should we just get jobs flipping burgers at McDonald's?"

"Ain't no future working for somebody."

I figured to just roll the dice.

"Tell me about Afghanistan, Shiner."

His face darkened.

"That ain't your business, Hap."

"But maybe you need help with that."

He glared, eyes bulging.

"Maybe you ought to just shut the fuck up."

I got him another beer.

"You'll feel better if you lift a phone, Shiner."

"I'm done with that penny ante bullshit."

"How much dough we got?"

He dug the wad from a pocket and tossed it to me. That was a first, letting me handle the take. I flipped through the bills. A couple grand. And what I had from pawning phones behind his back. I slipped a couple hundreds from the wad. He didn't bat an eye. Another first.

"I'm going to gas up the truck," I said.

Shiner nodded without eye contact.

Outside, I sagged against the truck. It was cloudy and looked like rain, dark clouds drifting in. Smelled like it, too. Shiner taught me that, to smell when it might rain. But now Shiner was out of lessons to give. It felt like he was fast becoming dead weight. Afghanistan sat hard on his chest and wouldn't let him breathe.

I mulled the options. I could just do what had been percolating in my mind and hit the road and leave him behind. I think I came close to it just the day before. He'd do that to me if it was the day for it. He'd do worse if it came to that, too. It was maybe now down to who'd strike first. Two circling cobras? Well, shit, I don't much care for snakes.

Like the day before, I was tempted to just drive off and see where the road took me. As I gassed up the truck at a Sunoco down from the motel, I watched cars on the highway. A solid stream of them. I wondered how many of them had a Shiner weighing them down, slowing them down.

I stood there a minute, just staring at nothing much, after the gas hose clicked off and the first drops of rain pelted my head.

BE ALL YOU CAN BE

It's not like Shiner to let me drive. For starters, I think driving is his last bit of control in a world that left him behind when he got back from Afghanistan. So he said, anyway, that rare one time he mentioned coming back from the war.

"But don't get too used to it, Hap. You're just driving today. I feel like just riding, today."

"Why today?"

"Call it a trial run. But not forever."

I thought to myself that forever with Shiner was feeling day to day. Twice, I'd come close to chucking the whole pissant adventure and slipping away. Today, I'm trying Plan B. I pull into the strip mall where the Army recruiter office is. I park right up front by its door. I see Sgt. Brodsky at his desk. He glances up but then back down at his paperwork.

Shiner sees the sign – Be All You Can Be -- and shoots me a surprised look.

"Wha's this bullshit, Hap? I done did my time – been there, done that, asswipe."

"That's a new one," I said.

"What is?"

"Asswipe. Goes on the list of banned words you can't call me anymore."

"You're slowly whittling away the English language."

"Just the ones you don't need no more."

"Says who?"

But then Shiner looks again at the sign and then at Sgt. Brodsky, who doesn't look up as he writes something.

"He looks like a right proper bullhead," Shiner said, smirking. "The shaved head, ramrod straight back. I bet he irons his boxers."

"That's Sgt. Brodsky."

"I wouldn't care if he was fucking Gen. Patton himself. And how do you know him?" He glances at me and then at the sign. "Fuck me -- did you come here to enlist, Hap? Is that what this shit's about."

"No. I didn't enlist. Ain't figuring to."

"Because you can't."

"Says who?"

"Says reality -- we're wanted in a million states for swiping smart phones, dickface."

"Dickface," I said. "I think you've used that one before. Very descriptive. But it goes on the list."

"Fuck the list and the horse it rode in on."

"Talk to Sgt. Brodsky."

"About what? How to steal smart phones?"

"Afghanistan."

Shiner looked in at Sgt. Brodsky still writing something.

"You saving my soul, Hap?"

"You even got one?"

"Everybody's got one," he snarled. "Doesn't make them all good."

"Whatever that means. Go talk to him. I told him you're a vet."

"And did you tell him how we make a living?"

"He don't know me from dick. I gave him a fake name. But he said you might need help. He offered."

"What do you get out of this, Hap?"

I shrugged.

"Maybe both our souls get saved today. I don't know. Just talk to him. Swap war stories. Do what vets do."

Shiner sighed. He stared at Sgt. Brodsky while I gripped the steering wheel, not sure if this was even a good idea. But Shiner's come close to wasting people and that's maybe a death sentence for us both if it happens with me around.

I'm surprised when I hear his door open, but he sits a few seconds, half in, half out. I'm tempted to nudge him on, but I know better than to suddenly touch him from behind. He's wound tighter than a spring.

"All you got to do is talk to him, Shiner. That's all."

"Easy for you to say."

But he eases on out and goes in. Sgt. Brodsky stands and offers a hand. They shake and Shiner glances over a shoulder at me. Sgt. Brodsky towers over him. I start the engine and back up slowly. I don't want to spook Shiner. I glance back once, at Shiner and Sgt. Brodsky across from each other at the desk.

I think, this might really be the end of it. Finished for good and ever. The other day when I nearly got to the interstate before turning back was maybe just a false start. A trial run.

Recon – that's what Shiner would call it.

Now I'm there, merging with traffic headed north from Memphis. I see a sign for Chicago, hundreds of miles ahead. But it don't quite sit right, what I'm doing. I know I ought to just keep going. That would be the smart move. Shiner wouldn't turn back if he'd got this far.

But I ain't Shiner. I don't even much like the man, but he pulled me off the streets when maybe my time wasn't far off from ending. So, I turned off and made my way back and looked in: Shiner and Sgt. Brodsky were shaking hands.

Something brought me back, and I need to know what it is.

We always must know, to see if it makes any difference, even though we suspect it won't at all.

TITANIC

It's been two days since Shiner talked to Sgt. Brodsky at the Army recruiting office. He hasn't said how it went. He didn't even ask where I drove off to while he was there. I think waiting for him to clue me in is like expecting the Titanic to come sailing over the horizon. That ship done sailed.

Am I still on it?

I think about where I'd be now if I'd just kept going the other day. Chicago, I suppose. But that's a pricey town. I don't know nobody there. And I remind myself all I know how to do is swipe smart phones and pawn them with Shiner. That's fueled us now for months and we do all right at it.

But thieving means city to city, not lingering long in one place, and living off pizza and Asian food in funny little cartons. Maybe some cheap Mex food. I do like them huevos rancheros. But is there a point to what we do?

"A point?" Shiner says. "You want a fucking point?"

"Yeah."

"Okay—what kind of point?"

"Why we do it."

"To survive, Hap."

"Maybe you could be more specific."

"To eat. That specific enough?"

"I hear you. Eating's good. What else?"

"How about warm motel beds? Or do you prefer to sleep in the truck?"

"But what's the end game?"

"Jesus," he said. "End game? That's a fancy fuck thing to say."

"Isn't there always an end game?"

"Do you think people like us get end games?"

"What about morality?"

He shook his head.

"It's just a word."

"But isn't it, like, an idea to live by?"

"Fuck morality. Somebody made all that up to separate people."

I reckon I'd never questioned any of it, the morality. Certainly not at the start. I think for me, morality was not an option when I was homeless. Homeless is morality-free. Going with Shiner was just changing one scene for another, a warmer one with better food.

Now, I reckon morality is in play after all. I've done things. I know that. Crimes. I did some when I was homeless. To live. What's the difference? Now, I see I have a choice. Like maybe I might have options. Even – worth. I just never had much chance to find it. I sat down on the bed opposite Shiner's.

"Goddamn it, Shiner – tell me what the fuck happened in Afghanistan."

"Go fuck yourself, Hap."

"C'mon, man – tell me."

"Turn on the damn TV if you want to hear voices."

He hung his chin on his chest a moment and then, surprisingly, sobbed.

Like a little hungry baby.

He went on like that for a minute or two and I guess I knew to just shut up and let it play out. That and I really didn't know what to say. I didn't know why I wanted to know these things. Just that I had to. Maybe because I'd stuck it out on this long road to nowhere, I owed it to myself to at least understand it.

"There was this boy," he finally said, wiping his eyes, his voice squeaky.

"The enemy," I said. "In Afghanistan."

"No. Just a boy. A punk kid."

"But not the enemy?"

"Just a pup in grimy white trousers too big for him."

"How old was he?"

"The runty bastard couldn't have been more than thirteen. If that."

"What about this boy, Shiner?"

"I shot him, Hap."

He said it so quietly, so calmly, that I drew back and felt like there might not be much left inside him but darkness.

"Why'd you shoot him?"

"There was a rifle, leaning against a wall. And that boy with a soft face, like a girl's face, standing there beside it."

"What was he doing there?"

"Just watching us troop by. I was the last man in – watching our six."

"And then you just shot him?"

"He put his hand on that rifle, Hap. Okay? I told him, 'I said, 'boy, don't you fucking do it.' But he picked it up and I brought mine up and aimed it square at his head. He wasn't more than six feet away."

"Did you give him a chance, Shiner?"

"More than anybody would have. But he raised it on up anyway and I shot him twice. His head exploded against the wall. Blood soaked into his baggy white pants and shirt."

He coughed hard several times and looked down into his hands and then clasped them in his lap, like he might pray for forgiveness. Shiner cried some more and covered his face with both hands.

"Well, shit," I said.

Now I knew. He hadn't really done nothing wrong, to my way of thinking. But I don't reckon right and wrong was the issue. It was maybe knowing he had to do it even though he knew it was kind of a death sentences for them both. Quick death for one, slow death for the other.

The death of Shiner's soul.

Shiner was dead man walking and so was I if I didn't get out soon, before I became that boy forcing his hand.

THAT'LL BE THE DAY

Now I'm doing the driving. For now, anyway. Shiner don't have the right focus for it since he fessed up about his Afghanistan crimes. I reckon that all he'd kept buried was now uncaged and wild and free and he must figure out how to live with it. I don't know that he's up to the task.

We're in northern Arkansas, Memphis in the rear view. Shiner ain't saying much. He tried the radio dial once but gave up because he didn't find any rock and roll – no Buddy Holly, no King Elvis. His favorites, I reckon. The ones he can talk about with a little bit of light behind his dead eyes.

He just looks out his window, his head lolled to a side against it. I glance at him and see where his breath makes a foggy spot on the window. We stop for gas in some shitburg named Fordyce, and after I pump it and pay, I lean against the truck and let the warm sunshine kiss my forehead.

Shiner's in the men's room. That gives me pause. He's out of sight. Maybe just for a few minutes. But with Shiner, you never know. He's still got that .44 magnum and I worry he's a man soaked in gasoline just looking for the match.

After a while, I see him come out and go inside the convenience store. I know he's got that .44 cannon in his waistband. I saw him take it out of his bag back at the Memphis motel. I didn't say nothing. I don't know that it would have done any good. Might have even got me killed. I'm not happy with my choice, but it's the one I made.

Now Shiner's loose in a convenience store in the middle of Redneck, USA, dragging his cannon around and that sets off alarms in my head and I start the engine and – freeze. I lock up for a moment, my mind unwilling to move forward. I don't know what to expect but I won't be surprised if I hear shots. Maybe this is the day Shiner makes his last stand. Maybe he's now back in Afghanistan.

Then where the fuck am I?

In my head, I hear a line from a Buddy Holly song, from when we visited the Holly center in Texas: "You say you're gonna leave, You know it's a lie, Cause that'll be the day, When I die"

I'm thinking this might be that day.

It's quiet in the store. I don't know how much time's gone by. Not much, I think, but it feels like normal time's flown off and life has down shifted to slow-motion. But I manage to unclog my head some and I put the truck in gear.

But what comes next? This is a moment, I understand, where there's more than one road to choose but all lead into darkness. I ease the truck across the lot, to right by the highway out of town. A quick getaway, if that's the choice.

But I can also just hit the gas and tear down the road and Shiner's a bad memory. Maybe he gets himself killed in there and that's that and I hear it on the radio by the time I reach Texas. But if Shiner lives, it don't matter how far away I am because I'll still be standing there right beside him, the burning gasoline spilling off him onto me, too. Two roasted dumbfucks.

Then I see a police car come up the highway and turn into the lot and I shiver, even though the sun has warmed up the cab. The cop gets out and as he opens the store door, Shiner comes through it. I want to just close my eyes tight and wish it all away, but something makes me watch. The cop asks Shiner something, and my eyes narrow. Here it comes. Shiner's hand eases up over his jacket. His cannon's underneath. I feel paralyzed.

But after a few words between them, the cop goes on in and Shiner slides into the truck. I stare at him, but he takes no notice. He rips open a bag of Frito's.

"Motherfucker, Shiner," I said, slamming my hands hard on the wheel a couple times.

"And just what's got the bee under your bonnet?" he said as he munched his Fritos and stared out the window. I put it in drive and we slipped onto the highway. After a while he offered the bag to me, and I grabbed a handful.

I always did like Fritos.

HALOS

Shiner drank himself to sleep and I needed some fresh air. We'd been cooped up in the motel, the TV offering the only words while Shiner stayed in his head figuring how to score cash without just swiping smart phones again.

I went out and walked down the street but there was no place I was going, just walking. The moon glowed full and bright and looked like I could just reach up and grab it. There was a church at the end of a block. It was built of grey stone with a tall pointy spire topped by a large cross. There were lots of tall stained-glass windows.

I supposed the figures with circles over their heads in those tall windows must be angels. I couldn't think of the word for those circles. I don't know anything about all that. I'd never been in a church. I can't say if angels are real. Above my pay grade, Shiner would probably say.

The massive church door wasn't locked. I went inside, figuring it must be okay, that I wasn't violating anything sacred. It was quiet inside. Dead quiet. Lifeless. A long red carpet led to the pulpit and a table with lots of lit candles. Their flames shimmered. Those flames waved like they beckoned to me.

I ran my hand over a flame and felt it tickle my palm. I liked the smell of the burning wax. On a wall, Jesus was on the cross and looked none too happy about it. He kind of sagged away from the cross. It looked painful. He had a solid complaint, for sure.

I didn't know what kind of church it was. I don't know Catholic from Muslim or any others. They're just words to me. Nobody ever drummed faith into me. One of my foster homes claimed to be Catholic and the other Baptist. I didn't stay at either one long enough to know the difference. They weren't churchgoers, those families.

I sat in a row and ran my hand over the smooth wood of the back of the pew in front of me. The wood had a pleasant odor. I don't know what it was. I recall that cedar smells good, but that's not what I'm smelling, and besides, cedar is light. This wood is thick, dense -- strong.

A man in a flowing black robe emerges through a door to the side of the pulpit. It kind of startles me some. He just appears sudden-like. I look to see if his feet touch the floor and chuckle at the thought. He's just a man in a black dress, basically.

"Good evening," he says, smiling.

"Evening."

I smile, too, but I don't know what to call him.

"How may I be of service, son?"

I hadn't thought about it going this far.

"I don't rightly know. The door was open – it's okay for me to be here, aint it?"

"Of course, son. God welcomes you."

I nod and glance over at Jesus on the cross and he don't look all that welcoming.

"I was taking a walk and now here I am."

"Journey's end, perhaps?"

I feel vaguely uneasy.

"Just a walk. No real journey to it."

"And yet you ended up here."

"Is that fate?"

"Do you believe in fate, son?"

I could see he was one of those that answer questions with questions. I supposed that was how churches worked.

"Fate's just a word, I reckon."

He nodded and frowned. Maybe I'd stumped him.

"What can I help you with, son?"

I looked again at Jesus. I saw more pain in his face each time.

"Well, I do have a question."

"Of course, son. Ask away."

"What do you call those circles over people's heads? In the windows, I mean."

"Halos."

"Are they angels, those folks?"

"And saints, too."

"What's the difference?"

"Angels are spirits without bodies. Saints once had bodies."

That didn't seem so clear to me. I figured I'd skip asking about spirits.

"I see. Well, that's good to know."

I stood. I wasn't sure if I ought to offer a hand and so I kept them at my side.

"Off so soon, son?"

"But one more question – what does a halo mean for them angels and saints?"

"It's the grace of God, a circle of light shining on them."

"Okay," I say, nodding, smiling. "That's kind of cool. A circle of light."

Out on the street, I glance up at the bright, glowing moon. I see it's a circle of light, too, like them halos. But when I think of those smart phones we swiped and how we'll just do it some more, I look again at the moon and see it's not a halo anymore.

FINDERS, KEEPERS

Shiner got it in his head to swing by the Crater of Diamonds. There was a sign for it after Arkadelphia, and it was right on our way because we weren't really going anywhere specific. We didn't have a clue about specifics, maybe New Orleans for a while, but for now we'd decided to see what the diamond place was about. We were low on cash, as usual, and needed a way to score.

When we got there, just outside Murfreesboro, it was like a family day at the diamond park. Lots of noisy kids and barking dogs ran loose. Some tour buses with old folks using canes and walkers drove up and unloaded. There were pickups with Confederate flags on the bumpers. Good old boys in faded coveralls. They'd all come out to see if they could strike it rich.

Light rain fell that morning. I heard somebody say rain loosened the soil to help reveal diamonds.

We listened to a park guy drone on about how old the place was, when the first diamonds were found, how to go about it in the huge field we were all about to get set loose in. That's where the diamonds are if there are any today. I was skeptical. I reckoned that if it was so damn easy, we'd all be rich.

"Finders, keepers, folks," the park guy said cheerfully. "Have at it."

The crowd buzzed like a gazillion bees huddled together.

"I'm going to find me a diamond, sure as shit," Shiner said, rubbing his hands together.

I worried that his .44 magnum was tucked into his waist, as usual. I leaned in close and whispered.

"Now, you wouldn't be packing that big cannon, are you, Shiner, out here with all these fine folks?"

He frowned and walked off, glancing back.

"Left it in the truck, Hap," he said. "You don't need no damn cannon to dig for diamonds."

We dug in this huge plowed field the park kept for the good tourists to chase their dreams. Nearby, some kid's dog took a dump. It left a steamy load and the stink washed over us in a breeze.

"That ain't right," I said.

"Maybe no diamonds over there," Shiner said, chuckling. "But be my guest."

We rooted around in that field, like so many others of all ages. I saw an old lady with blue hair helped down off her walker, to her hands and knees, so she could dig the earth like a dog looking for a bone. She went at it with both hands.

"That your grandma over there, Hap?" Shiner said, his own hands busy uprooting and sifting soil.

"Fuck you, Shiner."

"Yeah? Fuck me? You won't be so damn smart once I get my diamond."

I left Shiner to it and got a Coke at a concession stand. The park guy stopped by.

"Your buddy's hard at it, friend."

"He's a believer, I reckon."

"Ain't you?"

I shrugged but smiled.

"All I've seen so far is some dog shit."

"Roses live among thorns," he said, walking off with a smile.

I got a couple hot dogs and Cokes. We ate there in a row, folks all around digging like crazed, busy beavers. But everybody avoided where that dog took its dump. After we ate, Shiner went over there and rooted around. He waved.

"No, thanks," I said. "I'm good right here."

"Your loss," he said.

"Your dog shit."

He flipped me the bird and dug. Furiously. I imagined him digging his own grave. Maybe mine, too. We'd been one step ahead of the law now for so long that I reminded myself luck eventually runs out.

Then Shiner waved again. He was excited, holding something up in a hand.

"No, thanks," I said. "But keep all the dog turds you like."

He tromped over, staring at his hand. There was something yellow in it, with jagged edges. Maybe the size of a marble.

"Well, I'll be gone to hell," the park guy said. "You've got a winner there, fella."

"It's real?" Shiner said. "A diamond?"

"Yep. It's your lucky day. You got some money there once a jeweler's done with it."

We drove off, Shiner back to doing the driving, still no specific direction in mind. New Orleans was still an option.

"Maybe Baton Rouge first," Shiner said. "We'll find a jeweler there and see what's what with this rock."

I said, "Damn, Shiner. Looks like we've done gone straight."

"Don't be too sure about that."

I remembered the park guy said the diamond field lies over a dead volcano. I glanced at Shiner. His volcano, the one that grew inside him in Afghanistan, still rumbles, deep down inside him, the lava percolating.

It was just a matter of time.

WOLF MOON

Shiner was over the moon about the diamond he'd dug up back at the park in Murfreesboro. So much so that instead of just plowing down the road toward New Orleans, we took a room in Texarkana just so Shiner could sit on his bed and admire the little yellowish rock. He tossed it in the air and caught it, like a kid would a marble. I'd never seen him so relaxed since I'd known him, which was only a few months, but now felt like a lifetime. A lifetime that had gone on too long.

"What do you figure to do with it, Shiner?"

He caught it again and looked at me, surprised.

"It's a diamond, Hap. What do you think I aim to do?"

"Make yourself a ring?"

"Ain't you just the comedian," he said, tossing and catching his rock again.

I watched him do that a while. He finally missed and the diamond rolled under a bed.

"Careful you don't break your damn diamond, Shiner."

"Diamonds can't break, Hap. Don't you know anything?"

He still lacked the ability to hear when I was fucking with him.

"I know it don't look like any diamond I ever saw."

"You ain't never seen no diamonds, Hap. Not like this one."

"Yeah? Why's that one so damn special?"

"Because it ain't been refined yet. It has to be cut, you see? This here is straight out of mother earth in its natural state."

I nodded.

"How much you reckon it's worth?"

He held it up to the light.

"I can't rightly say. But a shitload, I reckon."

"And it's honest work, too, that diamond."

He gives me this look, like somebody trying to understand a foreign language.

"What's honest got to do with it?"

His eyes narrowed, and he got the usual cold blue eyes stare. I handed him an icy Bud out of the cooler.

"Ease up now, Shiner. All I'm saying is it's the first honest way we've scored.'

"Fuck honesty."

I nodded.

"I'm just stating a fact, that's all."

He tossed the marble again and snatched it quick-like, like a shortstop nabbing a hot grounder.

"Here's a fucking fact for you, Hap. A score's a score, honest or not. Stealing smart phones or finding a diamond – it's all the fucking same."

I knew I was hearing his morality statement, which was that it mostly didn't exist for him.

"If you say so," I said.

"I do say so, Hap. How about them apples?"

"You know, we could just go back to that park and look for more diamonds."

"We could," he said, tossing and catching the rock again. "But we done beat the odds with this one, Hap. Our number might not pop again for years. Maybe never. This here beautiful little baby was maybe one a in a million. No different than playing a lottery."

I nodded and sipped beer. Shiner held the rock in an open hand. He couldn't take his eyes off it.

"We could take the money and go to Mexico," I said. "It'd go far down there. Huevos rancheros for breakfast every damn day."

I was tossing out notions I knew I really didn't believe in. He stared at the rock like maybe he could somehow climb inside it and become part of it.

"I don't speak no Mexican, Hap. I don't care to learn."

Right then and there I knew for a fact that Shiner could not change. His damn diamond could be cut and refined and made beautiful and gleaming. But Shiner could not be made into anything but what he was: a raw volcano looking for a place to erupt.

The lava would fry me, too.

I went to the window and stared into the night, but there was a full moon, a wolf moon, I'd heard it could be called. There were no howling wolves outside that I could hear, just the one lone and gray wolf on a bed with a diamond tightly clasped in his hand, his eyes shut like he's nowhere at all except inside his own skin. No universe beyond his skin.

I sighed up at that wolf moon and figured Texarkana didn't feel quite right for abruptly jumping off a runaway train with a rabid wolf at the wheel. New Orleans sounded better. Bigger. More possibilities. Easier to get lost in, to elude a wolf. We could be there by tomorrow late if I kept Shiner on task. And I needed more time to work my nerve up.

It really was now down to the last opportunity for one of us to kill the other.

BUSTED FLAT IN BATON ROUGE

I woke up to Janis Joplin's whiskey raw voice on the radio. Shiner turned south toward Baton Rouge, maybe remembering I'd urged going to New Orleans. That's where I figured to make my getaway from him, which I'd aborted as far back as Memphis. I had this notion our luck was a frayed thread ready to snap. South of Natchez we pulled into a gas station to stretch our legs.

I went to the men's room and splashed water on my face. I made goofy faces in the mirror, just for the hell of it, when I heard the shots. First there was Shiner's .44 Magnum, and then a loud boom I knew came from a shotgun. We didn't have one. My face in the mirror didn't look like me.

The shooting seemed over as I eased around a corner. Shiner was face down by the station door, blood spreading from what was left of his head, and the station attendant, an old man with a bald head, sagged dead against the door, the shotgun across his lap, blood pouring from a wound in his neck. Smoke curled from the shotgun's barrel, like it had been smoking a cigarette. I shuddered, felt suddenly cold in the heat. All along, I feared I'd be the one that'd have to do it. Then I felt relieved I'd been spared that duty.

But I reminded myself I'd gone along willingly. I wasn't innocent. I was no hostage. I'd traded homeless and clueless back then for comfort, for adventure. But I never bought in to Shiner, I told myself. I wanted to believe that. I needed to believe that.

Well, now it was finished.

I sighed and stared at his shattered, bloody head, at the blue eye that hadn't been obliterated by buckshot. The other eye dripped bluish jelly. He seemed so much smaller now than I'd ever seen. And pitiful to look at. A mess of shattered humanity.

I went through his pockets and found the diamond, the one in a million score, he called it, from that diamond park in Arkansas. It didn't seem like more than a yellowish rock to me as I slipped it into my jeans pocket. It felt like it had no weight at all. I couldn't quite get what the big deal was over a diamond.

But, finders, keepers, losers, weepers. Shiner would probably have appreciated that.

I looked around the lot and listened for sounds, voices, but there was nobody else around. I fished a wad of cash out of one of his pants pockets. I glanced at him one last time. It no longer looked much like Shiner.

But I didn't feel sorry for him. Now, I'm not unfeeling, but I hadn't known him long enough to feel much at all. No tears.

He'd of felt the same about me. Even less.

His gun was beside him. There was blood on it. A drop dripped along the barrel. I kicked the gun away and went inside the store, careful not to touch anything. I didn't see any cameras. It was just a country store with an old type of register. The modern world hadn't caught up to that place yet.

What the fuck had Shiner been thinking? I shook my head. Jesus H. Christ. He had that diamond, that one in a million score in his pocket, and yet he tried to knock off a mom-and-pop store and his luck ran out. He couldn't stop himself, I reckoned. That simmering volcano inside him that got planted when he was in Afghanistan finally erupted and burned him up.

The till was open, and I could see the cash. Not so much, from the look of it. A few small bills, some coins. Not a haul at all. That was likely as far as Shiner had got before the man brought the shotgun up and Shiner probably dove back out the door. It seemed like a scene from a movie, like from Bonnie & Clyde. I wondered which of us was Bonnie and which was Clyde.

I grabbed a bag of potato chips and a Mountain Dew out of a cooler. Some cheese dip, and a bag of cashews, too, and I went out. There were no people, no cars. It was like this was the only place that existed, that the volcano inside Shiner covered the world in lava and I was the only survivor. I started the truck and just listened to the engine idle for a moment. It had a nice rhythm to it. Steady.

I glanced at Shiner and the other guy. It was like an old back and white photograph in a dusty book. I finally drove south, toward New Orleans, twisting the radio dial, but there was no Janis Joplin. All I got was Cajun caterwauling, some mournful Hank Williams. Janis was nowhere to be found. I tossed the empty Mountain Dew and chips bag out a window and saw the bottle bouncing along the road in the rearview mirror.

I found a likely place to ditch the truck and walked into the French Quarter with warm sun on my neck. I disappeared in the St. Patrick's Day crowd on Bourbon Street. I drank a few beers at a titty bar with frigid AC. It was as if none of it had ever happened, that Shiner had never happened. I tried to picture Shiner, but he wouldn't come into focus. He was just a smoldering mass fading away. A human consumed by lava.

Outside the bar, a man claimed the prettiest girls in the world were inside. I'd seen what they had, and it wasn't nothing to bark about on a sidewalk. I smirked and walked away, quickly swallowed up by a crowd, a great moving, colorful mass, and people next to me and in front were out of focus. Just shapes with heads on them.

The crowd swept me along and closed in on me until I felt as if we were all just one beating heart teetering on the edge of the unknown.

ABOUT THE AUTHOR

Michael Loyd Gray is an invited member of the Society of Midland Authors and author of seven published novels and more than forty published stories. Gray's novel The Armageddon Two-Step, winner of a Book Excellence Award, was released in December 2019. His novel Well Deserved won the 2008 Sol Books Prose Series Prize and Not Famous Anymore garnered a support grant from the Elizabeth George Foundation in 2009. He is the winner of the 2005 Alligator Juniper Fiction Prize and 2005 The Writers Place Award for Fiction.

Gray earned a MFA in English in 1996 from Western Michigan University, where he was a Phi Kappa Phi National Honor Society scholar. He earned a bachelor's degree from the University of Illinois. For ten years, he was a staff writer for newspapers in Arizona and Illinois. He lives in Kalamazoo, Michigan, with two cats and a dozen electric guitars and roots for the Chicago Bears.

9 781958 728291